DOUBLE DECEPTION

Forced to impersonate her twin sister, Gail has to pretend at one moment to be the unscrupulous Karen, and then revert to being her own less brittle self. And all because of one man—Luke Prentis!

DOUBLE DECEPTION

BY
KAY THORPE

MILLS & BOON LIMITED
15–16 BROOK'S MEWS
LONDON W1A 1DR

First published in Great Britain 1985
by Mills & Boon Limited

© Kay Thorpe 1985

Australian copyright 1985
Philippine copyright 1985
This edition 1985

ISBN 0 263 75039 6

Set in Monophoto Plantin 10 on 11 pt.
01-0585 – 54750

Made and printed in Great Britain by
Richard Clay (The Chaucer Press) Ltd,
Bungay, Suffolk

CHAPTER ONE

IT was dark when Gail opened her eyes, and the bed was moving.

No, not the bed, she realised, as sense and sensibility began to return. She was lying on the rear seat of a car from the feel of it, a pillow beneath her cheek and a rug tucked about her. Having ascertained that much, her mind seemed to develop a blank spot. The last thing she recalled with any clarity at all was lifting a coffee cup to her lips.

Her head felt heavy when she raised it, her mouth dry as a bone. A pair of broad male shoulders rose above the driver's seat, their width emphasised by the sheepskin coat. The head above them was dark-haired, the latter cut clear of the collar. She heaved herself slowly and carefully into a sitting position, meeting the swift flicker of a glance through the driving mirror with mingled relief and puzzlement.

Her voice when she spoke sounded thick and very faintly slurred. 'Where are we going? I can't seem to . . .'

'It doesn't matter where we're going—only why,' came the contained reply. 'Remember Jeremy Richmond?'

Gail shook her head, brows drawing together as the dull ache momentarily sharpened. 'I don't know anybody by that name. In any case, I don't see . . .'

'You will.' The tone had hardened. 'Karen Greer is about to get her come-uppance!'

'I'm not . . .' Gail began automatically, then broke

off, her teeth catching her lower lip. 'What are you talking about?' she said instead.

'My brother is what I'm talking about.' He was speaking without turning his head, his gaze on the road ahead. Lit only by the beam of the headlights, it looked both narrow and lonely, stretching into infinity without sign of human habitation. 'Breaking up his marriage was bad enough, but throwing him over on top of it just about sums you up for what you are! A gullible fool he might be, but he deserved better than that!'

'I'm sure he did.' Her mind was spinning, trying to grapple with all the imputations. Playing for time, she added shortly, 'Are you his keeper?'

'Call me his guardian angel, if you like.' He glanced at her through the driving mirror again as she put up a hand to smooth her temple. 'Head aching?'

'Yes, it is.' Gail was doing her best to sound calm and collected. 'Did you give me something?'

'I put a powder in your coffee while you were fetching the sugar for me. A real sacrifice on my part considering I never normally touch the stuff.' The derision increased. 'You went off like a baby! Getting you down to the car without being seen was the hardest part.'

Gail still couldn't bring herself to accept that this was really happening. It was all too much like a nightmare. 'What time is it?' she asked, with another glance out at the darkened landscape.

'Just gone five,' he said. 'We'll be there before first light.'

'Where's there?'

'That doesn't come under the heading of necessary information. Just take my word for it that running won't help because there won't be anywhere to run to.'

She swallowed thickly, alive to the implied threat in that statement. 'Luke, you have it all wrong,' she said. 'I know it's going to take some understanding, but I'm not Karen.'

His laugh sounded harsh. 'Like hell you're not!'

'It's true!' She paused, forcing restraint. 'If you'll just let me explain.'

'Okay,' he said. 'Go ahead.'

Gail took a deep breath. 'Karen's my sister—my twin sister. I was just pretending to be her.'

His eyes didn't move from the roadway ahead. 'Why?'

'Private reasons. Private and personal. Nothing to do with this situation.'

'I see.' His tone was noncommittal. 'So you never even met my brother?'

Her hesitation was brief. 'I'm not sure,' she admitted. 'What does he look like?'

'Like me, only a few years younger.' There was still no particular inflection to his voice. 'You do remember what I look like?'

Gail ignored the question, biting her lip. 'Yes, I met him,' she admitted. 'He called round one evening about a week ago.'

'The same evening you gave him the brush-off.'

She sighed. 'I suppose that's right, except that I didn't know then what I know now. I thought he was just another of Karen's men-friends, and I'd had enough of trying to do the thing nicely. If I hurt your brother's feelings I'm sorry.'

'Not half as sorry as you're going to be.' The grimness was back. 'Did you ever consider taking up fiction writing as a sideline? With that much imagination you'd have a head start!'

The anger welling in her owed as much to guilt as indignation. 'I tell you it's the truth!'

'Say it a few more times and you might even convince yourself,' came the satirical comment. 'Only do it under your breath because I'm not in any mood to listen.'

There was no getting through to him. Gail was forced to recognise that much as fact. She slumped back in her seat, wondering numbly how she was going to get out of this mess. Not that she could really blame anyone else but herself for having landed in it in the first place . . .

Although she had always called the woman who had brought her up 'Mother', Gail had been aware for years that her real mother was still alive. They had been divorced when she was little more than a year old, her father had told her the day he considered her ready to hear the truth. It had been a bitter parting, with neither party ever wishing to set eyes on the other again. Much as she loved her father, Gail was never able to forget that her other parent hadn't wanted her. The knowledge was a gnawing ache deep in the recesses of her mind.

It had been around the time of her twenty-second birthday some six months ago that her facial resemblance to a certain up-and-coming young photographic model had first begun to draw comment from friends. Even then, it had taken her father some time to tell her the whole story. Learning she had a sister, and a twin sister at that, came as a shock she could scarcely assimilate at first. Separating the two of them had been wrong, he acknowledged with sorrow and shame, yet at the time it had seemed the sensible alternative to a long legal battle for custody. Although using the name Greer for professional purposes, Karen was still a Branstead by birth.

Gail had hesitated for more than a week before

finally making the telephone call that had changed her life. Karen's reaction had been much the same as her own initially, yet looking back there had been undertones even then. She had neither time nor desire to visit the father who had spurned her, Karen said in the end, but if Gail was willing to make the break she could guarantee her a new and exciting future. Gail's decision to take up the offer was not only due to her desire to be with her sister. For some time she had been conscious of a certain monotony in her lifestyle— of a restlessness which could find no appeasement in the Midlands town where she had been born. Sad but understanding, her father made no attempt to stand in her way, simply expressing the hope that both she and Karen would find it in themselves to forgive.

Karen's flat was situated in Kensington. Regardless of expectations, when the door opened Gail could only stand and stare at the girl framed there. It was like looking in a mirror, seeing the same wide-spaced green eyes gazing back at her, the oval face with its slightly pointed chin, the mouth just a fraction too wide. Only the hair was different, its honey-coloured length cleverly streaked to appear as if bleached by sunlight, the style side instead of centre-parted.

Karen was the first to break the silence, her smile suggesting an irony Gail failed to understand right then. 'Easy to see we share the same mother, if nothing else. Come on in. We have a lot to talk about.'

Gail waited until the door was closed before saying tentatively, 'Dad told me she married the man she left him for. I suppose he's the one you call father?'

'Used to.' The reply was without particular concern. 'They broke up ten years ago. She's married again since. They live in Scotland. How is he? Your father, I mean.'

'Your's too,' Gail rejoined softly, and saw the familiar mouth slant.

'There's more to being a parent than holding the title.' A sweep of one hand indicated the room ahead. 'I don't know about you, but I need a drink. Leave your case where it is. We'll see to it later.'

The sitting-room was small, but imaginatively furnished, the decor a subtle mingling of earth shades with a little crimson and gold. Seated in the comfortable curve of a low slung chair, Gail eyed her sister for a long, appraising moment, noting the superbly applied make-up, the perfect fit of her cream wool suit. The pale grey coat she herself had just taken off had cost a packet by her standards, yet there was no comparison in cut. Self-consciously, she smoothed the skirt of her jersey dress, picking off a couple of minute pieces of fluff.

The gin and tonic went some way towards restoring her equilibrium. Karen tossed off her own drink with somewhat alarming swiftness, and went to get a refill.

'Good for shock,' she commented over a shoulder as if sensing unspoken criticism. 'It's just beginning to catch up with me.' She turned, glass in hand, green eyes resting on Gail's face with an odd expression in their depths. 'Are you a fatalist?'

'I don't think so.' Gail waited, brows lifting inquiringly. 'Why?'

'A passing thought.' The other's tone lightened. 'You said on the phone you were a trained beautician. That gives you a good start. Did you ever do any photographic modelling?'

'Only in a very amateur fashion,' Gail confessed. 'For a local club.' Her smile denigrated the experience. 'Anyway, I'd say you already cornered the market in that line.'

Karen laughed, twirling the glass stem between long slim fingers. 'Hardly yet. I still have to break into the real big time jobs. They don't come easily.' She took another quick swallow from the glass, eyes over-bright. 'Which is what I want to talk to you about, even if it is a bit soon. I never could stand suspense!' The pause was brief but telling. 'How would you like to do your sister a good turn?'

This time it was Gail who laughed. 'If I can.'

'Oh, I'm sure you can. All it will take is a little nerve, plus some know how I can pass on in no time.'

Puzzlement creased Gail's forehead. 'What are you talking about?'

'Simple really. I'm asking you to step into my shoes for a couple of weeks—literally, that is. Size five?'

'Yes, but . . .'

'Don't let me down. It's too perfect.' Karen's whole face was lit by some inner glow. 'When you phoned that evening it was like the answer to a prayer! They say twins have some kind of telepathic communication. You must have known I needed you.'

Gail leaned forward and put down her glass on a chrome-legged table, her movements very deliberate. 'I think you'll have to make it a little clearer,' she said slowly. 'You can't mean what you seem to be suggesting.'

Her sister didn't turn a hair. 'I mean it, believe me. If I'm rushing you it's because I don't have it in me to be subtle about it.' She put down her own glass and came to sit on the table, taking both Gail's hands in hers as if to persuade her by sheer force of will. 'There's this man who wants me to go away with him. He's immensely rich and very attractive, but the main thing is he has the kind of contacts who could—and would if he asked it—promote me right up front. The problem is if I don't come through with my end of the bargain soon he might start losing interest altogether. That's why I pressurised you to get down here so fast.'

Gail shook her head, trying not to let the implications cut too deeply. 'So far as I can see, it's a straight choice. You either go with him or you don't.'

'It's a long way from being that simple. The Agency has several jobs lined up for me. Nothing big—what you might call bread-and-butter work—but if I walk out on them I could finish up being blacklisted.'

'Would that make any difference to these contacts you hope to make?'

'No.' The green eyes didn't flicker. 'Hope is the operative word. There's always the chance it won't work out that way.'

'But you're still willing to risk it?'

Karen lifted slim shoulders, mouth twisting a little. 'No one ever got anywhere without seizing opportunity. With you here to hold the fort for me my options would still be open. I haven't told anyone else about you. Not yet.'

Gail was silent for a long moment, searching her sister's face with doubt written clearly across her own. 'He'd have to know about me, wouldn't he—this man you're talking about, I mean. If he ever got to hear afterwards that you'd . . .'

'It wouldn't matter to him. In fact, he'd probably admire my enterprise.' Karen's tone took on vibrancy as she sensed a certain weakening. 'You can't turn me down, Gail. I won't let you turn me down! The only real difference between us is the hair, and that can be taken care of right here without anyone seeing us together. Drew leaves for South America in a couple of days. It just means lying low till then. My next job is on Friday. I can fill you in on all the wheres and whens before I go. There's absolutely nothing difficult about it. You'll be told exactly what's wanted at each session. Of course, I'll transfer enough money into your name to make you financially independent while I'm away.'

'What about afterwards when you do come back?' asked Gail, buckling despite herself beneath the sheer weight of pressure applied. 'Would you expect me to simply disappear again?'

'Of course not.' Karen's smile was warm with reassurance. 'If things work out as planned, I'll be in a position to open doors for you too in your own line— even to back you in opening your own salon eventually.'

'And if they don't?'

'Then we'd try another tack. Twins with our looks have a rarity value. The potential would be enormous. Either way, both our futures will be assured.'

It was impossible, Gail told herself dazedly, trying to be rational about it. The whole suggestion was crazy! Yet the temptation was right there alongside the doubt. She had wanted a change of lifestyle, hadn't she? What could be more adventurous than this? Impersonating her own sister for a week or two was surely going to harm no one. If looks was what it took she had the same qualifications. And afterwards . . . Her imagination soared. What did she have to lose?

'Do you have any peroxide?' she asked, giving herself no more time to think about it. 'You can start telling me what I need to know while we work.'

By midnight, when the two girls finally retired to bed, the transformation was complete. Looking at their faces reflected side by side in the mirror, Gail had been barely able to tell any difference herself. It was an odd sensation after so many years of considering oneself fairly unique, she acknowledged, yet there was a sense deep inside of completion, as if some missing part of her had finally come home. If she had any regrets at all it was in that she and Karen were so soon to be parted again, but it would not be for long, and they had a whole lifetime left to be together.

That they were two very different characters, she already knew. There was no way she herself could have contemplated the kind of transient affair Karen was embarking upon, no matter what the incentive. Not that she condemned her for it either. It was just the way she happened to be made. No, not made, a part of her mind corrected; formed would perhaps be a better word. Parted from such an early age, even twins must be influenced by environment. From what she had said during the course of the evening, Karen had experienced little stability in any sphere of her upbringing. Was it so surprising if she tended to grasp whatever life offered?

Regardless of everything, one day she was going to have to look up her mother again, reflected Gail. It wouldn't be an easy confrontation, but it was necessary to her peace of mind.

The two days flew. Gail scarcely stirred from the flat, spending her time memorising the various instructions Karen had written out for her and practising facial expression before a mirror until she finally grasped the art of letting the desired emotion come from within by using her imagination to paint pictures in her mind. There were moments when she desperately regretted becoming involved in the plot at all, yet with Karen already packed for her trip she hardly felt able to start backing out. Wakening on the Wednesday morning to find herself alone in the flat came as no real surprise. If there was anything at all in this alleged telepathic communication between twins, Karen would have sensed the danger.

The note left in a prominent position on the kitchen bar confirmed that notion. *Didn't want to risk a change of mind,* Karen had written in a sloping hand not all that much unlike Gail's own, *so I'm leaving early. Don't hesitate to draw on the account we opened. You'll be doing the work, you deserve the reward. See you whenever.*

The signature was a boldly scrawled initial *K*. Studying the few lines of script, Gail thought wryly that Karen's judgment had not been at fault. There was a highly probable chance that common sense might have gained the upper hand in the final moments. Too late now. Her bridges were burned. She would just have to hope she could carry it off. Both Karen's future and her own could depend on it.

The more immediate future proved to be even more difficult than she had anticipated, not so much in the work itself which she could and did imbibe as she went along, but in the personal relationships Karen had not seen fit to warn her about. Her sister's affairs, she discovered, were not only varied but in several cases concurrent. Disillusioned, she became practised at turning away puzzled swains, gently at first but with increasing ruthlessness as her patience evaporated. By the time Karen returned she was going to find herself with scarcely a man left in her life, yet Gail refused to feel any remorse. She had agreed to take over the job not the sleeping partners.

That apart, there were other moments when she found herself becoming confused as to which identity she was actually supposed to be assuming. Writing to her father and stepmother, she had to be prepared at any moment to make the switch in order to answer either door or telephone. References to Karen were of necessity guarded. Her father in particular would be horrified to learn the truth. Sometime in the not too far distant future he was going to want to meet his other daughter, there was nothing surer. Gail had to trust that Karen would be home before that happened, although there had been no word from her since her departure. The faint possibility that she may not return at all was not to be contemplated.

Even allowing for the clothing Karen must have taken with her, the wardrobes lining one wall of the bedroom were still far from empty. Some of the outfits Gail wore because they suited the occasion, others she discarded because they failed to cater to her own particular taste. Of the people with whom she came into contact during her working day, only Karen's personal agent was in a position to note any personality changes. Once or twice, Gail caught the woman eyeing her with a certain speculation, but no comment was ever made. Who without inside knowledge could possibly suspect the true situation? she asked herself wryly. One of the worst parts of this whole affair was going to be explaining the deception when the time came, although she doubted if any amount of personal disapproval would blind the Agency to future advantages if that was the way things went.

Karen's social life had been full in every sphere. Anxious to avoid too apparent a change in habits, Gail found herself going to parties almost every other night, and becoming rapidly adept at the facile repartee endemic to such affairs, although she felt the strain. Little of what she had so far experienced of her sister's world was living up to expectations. She was even having second thoughts about wanting to become a part of it. Her own line of work promised more fulfilment. Tired and bored one particular evening, she had retreated into a quiet corner for a few minutes and was wondering if anyone would really notice if she slipped away when she became aware of the man leaning against the wall a few feet away. At first glance there seemed an elusive familiarity about his features, yet to the best of her knowledge they had not met before. Grey eyes returned her gaze with equability—steel grey, she noted: impenetrable as the metal itself. His face was angular, the jawline strongly etched, with a cleft at the centre point of the chin. Thick dark hair fell in a comma over his forehead.

'Luke Prentis,' he said, answering her unspoken question. 'And you're Karen Greer. I saw your screen test for Apergé.' His smile stirred her responses. 'Very memorable!'

'But it didn't get me the job,' Gail rejoined, thankful that Karen had seen fit to mention the test.

'Only because you weren't quite the type they were looking for.' He hadn't taken his eyes from her face. 'Odd, but I'd have thought they'd have seen you had the potential to be whatever they did want. I've been watching you tonight. You can switch mood like a chameleon switches colour!'

And she had believed herself so firmly entrenched in her sister's shell, thought Gail wryly. This man was shrewd. She would have to watch herself.

'You're involved in TV advertising?' she asked.

'Only on the fringe. I write books for a living these days.'

Memory sprang to life. Luke Prentis. Of course! 'Fireball!' she exclaimed. 'You wrote Fireball.'

One dark eyebrow lifted a fraction. 'You've read it?'

'No,' she admitted. 'I'm not into male adventure. I do know it topped the lists for several weeks though— as did your last two books before it.' She studied him for a moment, considering the way her sister might have handled the conversation. 'A bit more than just a living, I'd have thought,' she ventured boldly at length. 'You're being modest, Mr Prentis.'

'Oh, come on.' His tone was lightly mocking. 'Who

stands on ceremony in this day and age? Make it Luke.
It sounds a whole lot friendlier.'

Gail smiled back at him, refusing to be put down.
'All right, Luke. And you may call me Karen.'

'Thanks.' There was a faint spark in the grey eyes.
'You know, beauty and sex appeal aren't always
synonymous, but you seem to have copped the lot.'

An answering spark leapt in her own eyes. 'Believe
it or not, I even have a brain!'

'I believe it,' he said, not turning a hair. 'I mightn't
have done before today, but having met you . . .' He
left the rest unsaid, the slant of his lips contracting her
stomach muscles. 'Are you as ready to get out of here
as I am?'

The suddenness of the question took her by surprise; she made an effort to collect her wits. 'Why?'

'I'd like to take you out to dinner.'

'It's almost ten-thirty.'

'Supper then.'

She let the pause stretch for a moment before
starting to shake her head. 'I don't think . . .'

'Then don't. Just say yes.'

'All right.' The agreement was dragged from her
regardless of will—or maybe because she simply didn't
want to say no; she wasn't sure which. 'Where?'

'Leave that to me.' He gestured towards the far side
of the crowded studio. 'Get your coat and I'll see you
out in the lobby.'

Gail went without further demur to do as he bid.
She had come in Karen's hip-length silver fox over
her own silky black dress. Registering the shine in her
eyes through the dressing-room mirror, she decided
suddenly that for tonight she was going to be herself
in everything but name, because it was as herself she
wanted to impress Luke Prentis. Tonight she was
going to take a single leaf out of Karen's book and live

for the moment, regardless of anything else. Let the future take care of itself.

Luke was waiting in the lobby as he had said. He was studying a notice board on the wall, his back to the studio doors, a sheepskin coat slung ready across a nearby chair. Taller even than she had realised, his breadth of shoulder was balanced by the length of his legs. Lean, lithe and wholly magnetic, was her mental summing-up. A man who attracted her as few others had. If at around thirty-two or three, he was also a few years older than any other man she had dated, then that simply added to the attraction.

Most important of all, she was bound to admit, was the knowledge that Karen herself had never been involved with him. This was her conquest; hers and hers alone, even if she was the only one to know it.

She was surprised though not particularly disconcerted to see the Range-Rover parked in the alleyway when they got outside.

'Sorry about this,' Luke said, seeing her seated before getting behind the wheel himself. 'My car's in dock and I hate using taxis unless I'm forced.'

'It's not exactly roughing it in this,' Gail laughed. 'I can always imagine we're going on safari!'

'Safer than braving London traffic anytime,' agreed Luke dryly, giving her an odd look. 'You're a regular bundle of contradictions.'

Perhaps that remark alone should have brought her up short, but it didn't. She was enjoying herself for almost the first time in more than two weeks. 'Never take anything for granted,' she said demurely as he fired the ignition. 'We all have more than one side to turn.'

They went to a small, intimate Italian restaurant somewhere off Piccadilly where Luke appeared to be well known. Conversation was free and far-ranging, opinions not always sympathetic. Once or twice Gail was aware of a seemingly deliberate pulling-up on Luke's part, as if he were reminding himself that argument, no matter how entertaining, was not what he had had in mind. Which begged the question of what he did have in mind, except that she didn't really want to consider the possible answer. There would be time enough to think about that if and when the need arose.

It was almost midnight when they pulled up outside the flats. After Luke had insisted on seeing her safely up in the lift, it seemed churlish not to ask him in for coffee before he made his way home. He spent the time while she made the drink looking over Karen's scant library of books, eyeing her with some disparagement when she brought in the tray.

'For someone who can think and talk the way you do, you read a whole lot of rubbish,' he commented bluntly. 'Didn't you tell me you weren't a fan of mine, by the way?'

Gail's eyes went to the bookshelf, only now recalling where she had last seen that paperback title. 'You call your own work rubbish?' she countered, playing for time as she deposited the tray on the low table.

'You know what I'm talking about,' he said. 'I write for a market I shouldn't have thought was in your line after tonight.'

'Maybe I need some light relief.' she responded without meeting his gaze, 'Or maybe I simply bought the book because I liked the cover and it helps fill a shelf. Cream or milk?'

'Neither.' She hadn't heard him move, but he was suddenly right there beside her, drawing her upright to find her mouth with his in a kiss that silenced any protest she might have been about to make. Without thinking about it, she slid her arms about his neck and kissed him back, lips parting to his urging, body softening to mould to his shape. If these past two weeks had given her anything it was confidence. There had been a time when a man like Luke Prentis would have scared her half to death.

There was something she couldn't fathom in his expression when he put her from him.

'You forgot the sugar,' he said.

It was warm in the car, yet Gail couldn't control the sudden little shiver. Luke Prentis was a ruthless man, capable of anything. His attraction had flown. She would be wasting her time making any further appeal to his better judgment. Where she was concerned, or more accurately, where Karen was concerned, he had already made up his mind.

'I assume the Prentis is a *nom de plume*,' she said. 'Unless your brother had a different father.'

'It's better box-office,' he agreed, ignoring the last. 'I thought you'd gone back to sleep.'

'I was thinking.'

'Working out some new line?' His tone was sardonic. 'Make it a bit more plausible than the last one, will you.'

Gail said stonily, 'I don't have anything to add.'

'That's a step in the right direction.'

'Will it do me any good?'

'Not so you'd notice.'

'Why are you doing this?' she burst out, momentarily losing her cool. 'What do you think you're going to achieve?'

'Satisfaction,' he answered. 'Jerry isn't the only one whose life you've turned inside out.'

'Is that established fact,' she demanded, 'or simply guesswork?'

'It's reputation.'

'Another word for gossip.' She made no effort to disguise the sneer. 'I'd have thought you above taking that at face value, or are you going to tell me there's no smoke without fire?'

His eyes lifted briefly to the mirror, derision visible even from where she sat. 'Ain't that the truth! Forget the brickbats. My hide's thicker than a rhino's.'

'That I can believe.'

'You'd better.'

Gail retreated into silence again, the better to marshal her reserves. It was still as black as pitch outside, moon and stars hidden away behind dark cloud. The time was just coming up to six o'clock. If they had been travelling since midnight, or there-abouts, they were almost certainly going north. But where? The landscape out there was far from flat, which ruled out Norfolk and most of Lincolnshire. In any case, after six hours they'd be further than that. Yorkshire, perhaps—or even Westmorland? She may have a better idea when daylight came to expose the terrain in greater detail.

Lights down in a valley drew her attention, but it was only a momentary glimpse before they were hidden again by the rising land. It could have been a small village just beginning to waken to the day, or maybe only a farm—whichever, it spelled civilisation. That was a comfort in itself.

The road they were travelling had grown narrower and steeper during the last fifteen minutes, now it started to drop again, curving the shoulder of the hill. A ridge stood out starkly across the valley against a slightly lighter band of sky. There came the sound of rushing water, a tiny, stone-walled bridge, then they were turning, bumping along a rutted track until the darker bulk of some kind of building loomed ahead.

Luke drew up in front of it, switching off the engine but leaving the headlights on dip.

'Welcome to Fellside cottage,' he said. 'I'll do my best to make your stay a memorable one!'

CHAPTER TWO

THE cold cut through Gail like a knife the moment she opened the car door. Shivering, she reached behind her for the thick tartan rug, pulling it about her shoulders as she slid her feet out on to stony ground.

'Try waiting,' Luke advised, already on his way to the cottage door. 'You'll break an ankle in those heels without a helping hand.'

'As if you'd care!' she flung after him. 'I don't need your help.'

'Suit yourself.' He had a key in his hand, secured from the lip of the doorframe. There was a grating sound as he inserted it in the lock, a creak of hinges as the door swung inwards. The darkness beyond was denser than that without. He vanished into it.

With little choice but to follow, Gail got out of the car and took a few steps, biting back the sharp exclamation as one heel cockled beneath her. Walking on her toes, she managed to make it across to the door, stepping inside to a temperature scarcely less frigid. Somewhere ahead of her a match flared, and a glow began to spread, revealing a small and sparsely furnished room.

She closed the door and stood with her back against it, her body so cold she thought she would never be warm again. 'Where's my coat?' she demanded, longing for the comfort of thick soft fur.

'We didn't bring it.' He sounded unapologetic. 'It would be out of place up here. There's a selection of stuff in the boot, including some slacks and sweaters.

Give me a chance to get the fire lit, and I'll fetch them in.'

A fire. That sounded better. Gail subsided into the nearest chair, kicking off her shoes to tuck both feet up under her, the rug clutched close. She wasn't moving from here until some creature comforts were established, and that was a fact!

There was a fire already laid in the open hearth. Luke put a match to it, waiting until the base paper had caught in several places before easing himself upright again. The crackling sound of flames licking at dry wood was warming in itself.

'There's food in the kitchen through there,' he said, dusting off his hands with scant regard for his tailored slacks. 'Take the lamp with you. I can light another. The stove's run off calor gas. There should be enough left in the cylinder to see you through breakfast.'

'If you think I'm going to cook and bottle-wash for you,' Gail said icily, 'you can think again!'

His expression didn't alter. 'Not just for me, for both of us. If I have to feed myself that's all I will be doing. You can fry bacon, I take it?'

'I can do a whole lot of things you wouldn't even credit,' she retorted. 'Including starving, if that's what it takes to show you I mean what I say.'

'You'll change your mind.' He sounded totally unmoved. 'Hunger's a great incentive.'

She waited until he had gone outside before getting to her feet to pad across the rug-strewn boards to the fire. A small wooden stool stood close by. Huddled on it as close to the now leaping flames as she could safely get, she at last began to thaw out. With warmth came the realisation of how she must look. Her hair felt a tangled mess, her eyes gummy with mascara, while the black dress was covered in bits of fluff from the woollen rug. Her stockings had ladders running up the front of both legs. Feeling the way she did about the man who had brought her to this state, it shouldn't have mattered, yet it did. Personal pride alone was sufficient reason.

The outer door flew back against the wall as he booted it open, admitting an icy blast of air. Arms full, he used a foot to shut it again behind him, dumping his load on the chair Gail had vacated. Sorting swiftly through the pile, he picked out a pair of beige corduroy pants and a thick blue sweater, tossing them across to her.

'Get into those and you'll feel better.'

'While you do what?' she demanded scathingly. 'Watch?'

His shrug bespoke indifference. 'Why the concern? It can't be any novelty to have a man around while you take off your clothes—or do they usually do it for you?'

The need to hit back was stronger than discretion. 'Would you like the details of your brother's preferences too?'

A muscle jerked in his jaw. 'Leave Jerry out of it.'

'How can I? He's what this is all about.' She hesitated when he made no immediate reply, searching the strong features for some sign of remission. 'Luke, it isn't too late to sort this whole thing out. All it needs . . .'

'All it needs is a change of tactics, is that what you're thinking?' He shook his head. 'There's no way I'm letting you off the hook, Karen, no matter how you play it. I brought you here for a purpose, you'll stay until it's been achieved. Get changed.'

If she didn't there was every chance he might do it for her. Clenching her teeth, Gail dropped the rug and rose from the stool, reaching a hand to the long back zip of her dress. Luke stayed right where he was, watching her dispassionately as she slid the garment down over her hips and stepped out of it. Beneath it she was wearing black lace briefs and skimpy bra, the thin bands of the four suspenders spanning the firm flesh of her thighs. She drew on the cords without hurrying, thrusting her arms and head into the blue sweater to emerge tousled but in command.

'From the skin outwards,' commented Luke with irony. 'That was quite a performance.'

And he would never know what it had cost her, she thought. If her pride was what he was after he was going to have a long wait.

The sky outside the two small windows was starting to lighten a little, the blackness turning a dull dark grey. She could see the stunted shape of a tree, and beyond it the vague jutting outline of a shed.

'If you won't tell me where this place is,' she said, 'at least tell me what.'

'It's where I come to get away from people,' Luke acknowledged, shedding the sheepskin. 'Admittedly, I've only used it before in summer when the lack of mod cons isn't quite so noticeable. There's water on tap from the stream, but it has to be boiled before drinking. No bathroom, just the lean-to you can see out there. A bit primitive, I agree, but nothing you can't get used to.'

Gail curled a lip. 'You perhaps, not me!'

'It's Hobson's choice. The man who laid the fire for me and stocked up with provisions lives twelve miles away, and he's our nearest neighbour. You may have noticed we're not on the phone either, so don't imagine you're going to be sending for help the minute my back's turned.'

'He knows you were planning on bringing me here?'

'He knows I was planning on bringing someone— could be he guessed it would be a woman.' He registered her fleeting change of expression with a faint dry smile. 'He's unlikely to suspect anything amiss. I'd say he subscribes to the opinion that writers, artists and musicians are all eccentrics anyway, and that includes the people they associate with.'

'But he's still willing to do things for you, obviously.'

'I pay him to do things for me. We've food and fuel enough to last a week if necessary.'

'A week!' Gail stared at him in horror. 'You're not eccentric,' she declared, 'you're mad! What difference is it going to make to anything dragging me off to this God-forsaken spot?'

'It's going to make you think twice before you break up any more marriages, for one thing,' came the grim return. 'You're too used to having things all your own way!'

Gail took a hold on herself, biting back the savage retort. She was already in trouble enough without antagonising him further. 'Did it ever occur to you,' she said after a moment, 'that your brother could have passed himself off as a single man?'

'Not true. He wore a wedding ring. He said you even asked him once what his wife was like.'

Not me, she wanted to deny, but what was the use? 'Naturally, he refused to talk about her,' she jibed instead.

Grey eyes took on a dangerous spark. 'I don't give a damn what he might or might not have said. You didn't care about him. He was just another scalp on your belt.'

'How old is he?' Gail demanded. 'Twenty-six? Twenty-seven? You'd be better employed trying to teach him to stand on his own two feet instead of running to big brother with his problems. If his wife threw him out it could be because it wasn't the first time he'd been unfaithful.'

'Brenda didn't throw him out,' he said harshly. 'The besotted idiot walked out on her and a couple of young children because he believed you'd have him if he were free. He got himself tied down too young, but he was content enough until you appeared on the scene. If he lost his head you helped him do it. Now he's lost everything.'

'I'm sorry.' It was the only comment she could make. 'I really am sorry, Luke.'

'Sure you are.' The scepticism lay heavy. He took a glance out of the window where distant hills were just coming into view. 'The forecast promised snow on high ground. From the look of that sky it won't be long in coming.' His gaze came back to her, losing none of its hardness in the process. 'Not that it's going to make a deal of difference. If anyone saw you leaving with me last night it might be assumed that we're together when you turn up missing, but no one's likely to guess where.'

Gail said slowly, 'I had a photo-call for eleven this morning which I'm obviously not going to make. Assuming that's part of the plan, do you really believe the unreliability label is going to stick once I do get back and explain the circumstances?'

His shrug made light of the threat. 'It would be your word against mine, for what it's worth. Seeing you blacklisted would be a bonus, I admit.'

'On top of what?'

'The loss of your big break.' The pause held deliberation. 'You see, I happen to know that Cassie Bailey broke a leg skiing yesterday, which means she's out of the Rivas contract. They've less than a week to find a replacement. Your name was top of the list.'

The fire was scorching the backs of her legs but she

didn't move, looking at him with eyes gone dark. She had picked up enough this past couple of weeks to know what he was talking about. The new Rivas perfume was due to be launched next month with a media coverage second to none. Just gaining the job alone had made Cassie Bailey a household name overnight. The ballyhoo likely to be raised in the appointment of her successor stood to surpass all. Not that it would have gained Karen anything had she chosen to stay in London—except that she might not have fallen quite so easily into Luke's trap.

'Nothing to say?' he mocked. 'That makes a change.'

Bitter words sprang to her lips but she caught them back, her mind leaping ahead. Supposing, just supposing Karen was on her way home right now—or even at the flat already? Of course, she had probably been speaking figuratively when she had said a couple of weeks, but there was always a faint chance that she might have set a time limit on her powers of persuasion. Whatever she had done, Luke Richmond had no right to be doing this! It would be simple poetic justice were he to fail in his aim.

'There's nothing I could say that would get through that hide of yours,' she retorted, keeping a firm grip on herself. 'Didn't you tell me that in the car? I'm neither going to waste my breath nor give you any satisfaction by even trying!'

Grey eyes sought to penetrate her control, narrowing to steely points. 'I'll say one thing for you, you're no cry-baby. Maybe as well considering. Want to get started on breakfast?'

'You can whistle,' she said flatly, and saw his shoulders lift.

'Your loss.'

He moved then, but not towards the far door,

searching through the heap of clothing to pull out a pair of jeans and a dark grey sweater that both looked as if they had seen better days. Gail ostensively turned her back as he slid off his jacket, looking into the leaping flames with fixed attention. Being stoic about things was all very well, but where did it leave her? She was trapped God alone knew where with a man who had already proved himself totally without scruples. One thing was certain, she had no intention of simply sitting back and accepting whatever else he might have in mind. Snow or no snow, the very first chance she got she was getting out of here.

She took the stool again when he went through to the kitchen, clasping her hands about her knees and trying to ignore the stirrings of hunger. There came the sound of a match being struck, the slight bang as gas jets took flame, the clatter of dishes then the sizzle of hot fat. The smell of frying bacon made her ache. Her mind's eye saw the rashers lying in the pan, the rind crisping and curling, the lean so mouth-wateringly pink. All she had to do was to go through and take over the pan. Was it such a big deal?

Self-disgust overcame the temptation. What was a little hunger compared with the degradation of knuckling under to that man in there? What she had to do was show him her will power was at least equal to his. He could hardly let her starve.

Regardless, it took every ounce of control she had to keep an impassive face when Luke brought through a loaded tray to the plain deal table. There was one plate, filled to capacity, one knife and fork, but two steaming mugs of coffee.

'Here,' he said, holding one of the latter out to her. 'I won't deny you a hot drink.'

Gail toyed briefly with the notion of tipping the contents of the mug on to the floor, but the aromatic smell was too much for her. A childish gesture, anyway, she reasoned, taking the mug from him. The eyes she lifted were schooled to show no hint of triumph.

'Thanks.'

The drink tasted wonderful, but did little for her empty stomach. She found her eyes following every lift of the fork, savouring every mouthful Luke took. If she felt like this now what was it going to be like by the end of the day? she wondered ruefully. Could she really last out long enough to break down his resistance?

But he had been driving all night, she recalled. Sometime soon he had to need sleep. If she hung on till then the problem might be solved without loss of face. It was a faintly cheering thought.

He cleared the plate without comment, pushing back his chair to prop a foot comfortably across the other knee while he finished his coffee. Gail could feel him watching her, but she refused to look up.

'It's been a long drive,' he remarked almost as if he had read her thoughts. 'The sofa there opens up into a bed. You'll just have to stay still and quiet while I catch up on what I missed last night.' The pause itself mocked her. 'Incidentally, the car keys are right here in my pocket, if you were thinking along those lines.'

'I wasn't,' she denied stonily, 'thinking along any lines.'

'Not much point,' he agreed. 'You'd have no idea which direction to take.'

Any direction away from this place would do, Gail told herself, ignoring the obvious drawbacks. Somewhere out there were people who would help her—the police if necessary. She wondered what Karen might do if she had returned and found her missing. The slacks and sweater she was wearing now were her own, as were several other items among the pile on the chair, but the rest of her stuff was still at the flat so it could hardly be imagined that she had gone back home. And there lay a further concern.

'How do you think my family's going to feel if I don't call them?' she asked, and saw his lip curl.

'The same way they've felt this last couple of years, I imagine. You told Jerry it was that long since you had any contact.'

She said caustically, 'Is there anything he didn't tell you?'

'Not a lot. He was in shock the night he arrived at my place after you'd given him the push. He wanted me to understand how he felt about you—why he'd imagined you needed someone.' Luke's tone had roughened. 'You couldn't even take the trouble to let him down gently, could you.'

The words were jerked from her. 'I already explained why I . . .'

'Not the twin sister bit again!' The force with which the empty mug met the bare wood of the table was indicative of his frame of mind. 'What kind of a fool do you think I am? You never even had a sister!'

'It's a long story.'

'Oh, I'll bet it is. And you've had plenty of time to perfect the detail.' There was scorn in the glance he raked over her. 'Don't add insult to injury!'

'The injury wasn't yours to start with,' Gail pointed out, giving up the attempt to reason with him. 'That's probably just an excuse!'

Grey eyes narrowed. 'For what?'

'Indulging your kinky habits.' The need to pierce that unfeeling hide of his blinded her to everything else. 'I've heard about men like you. Bondage, it's called, isn't it?'

He seemed an age coming to his feet. Heart

thudding against her ribs, she watched him move towards her, fighting the instinct to shrink from him. The hand dragging her upright from the stool was hard as iron. Pinned against the wall at her back, she suffered the relentless pressure of his mouth, feeling her lips yield to a force greater than her strength of mind. There was no escaping the lean and muscular body; he had her blocked in every direction. Her thighs buckled beneath the crushing weight.

She would have slid nervelessly down the wall when he drew away had he not kept that same iron grip on her upper arms. His eyes were blazing still, his breathing heavy, but he had command of himself.

'If I intended using you at all, I wouldn't need to tie you up to get satisfaction,' he gritted. 'Truth is, there've been too many there before me—including my own brother!' A muscle contracted suddenly in his jaw as he looked down into her face. Abruptly he released her, raking back the comma of dark hair with a forceful hand. 'Cool it,' he advised. 'There's more than one way to skin a cat.'

Gail could believe that. Where this man was concerned she could believe anything! The tremors still running through her were not wholly due to fear. For a moment there he had reached a part of her that had wanted to respond regardless. The contempt in his voice had cut deep. Not me, she wanted to scream at him. It wasn't me! Pride alone kept her silent. He wasn't going to believe her no matter how many times she said it. Why demean herself by appearing to plead?

She stayed where she was as he moved across to pull out the sofa-bed. It was less than a double in width, the mattress already made up with sheets and a single blanket. Luke took pillows from a cupboard nearby and tossed them down, glancing briefly her way.

'There should be enough logs in the box there to keep the fire going,' he said. 'If you did run out before I wake up there are plenty more under the tarpaulin round the back.'

Her voice sounded strained. 'You can sleep under these conditions?'

'I can sleep under any conditions when I need to,' he came back dryly. 'Night driving is pretty exhausting. Turn the lamp out, will you. It's light enough now.'

The sneakers he had donned along with the jeans and sweater were the only things he took off before sliding between top sheet and blanket. Lying there on his side with one arm upcurved across the pillow, he looked perfectly relaxed. When, bare moments later, his breathing smoothed and deepened, Gail could hardly believe it. That was as much as all this meant to him!

Resisting the automatic impulse to tiptoe, she went over and turned out the oil lamp, finding the cold greyness of daylight a deal less comforting. There was snow up there for certain, she thought, looking out of the window at the lowering cloud. What she could see of the view was bleak and desolate, the slope of hillside on which the cottage stood extending down to a narrow valley backed by further rugged slopes. There were trees in the bottom, and a glimpse of water beyond, but no sign of other habitation. The Range-Rover that had brought them here stood sentry at the top of a rough track vanishing out of sight around the shoulder of the hill. Apart from a short section of dilapidated fencing, the cottage occupied no designated area of land. If there had ever been a garden at all it had been allowed to return to nature.

With clear visibility down to less than half a mile, Gail couldn't be sure if the lower end of the valley opened out or closed right in. Not that it was so terribly important anyway, except that a wider view might have given her some clue as to their whereabouts. If she was to leave here on foot it had to be via the track, because that was the only way she could be certain of finding her way out. Twelve miles from their nearest neighbour, Luke had said, but he didn't have to be telling the truth, did he? Those lights she had seen had been closer than that, she was fairly certain.

He was still lying in the same position when she turned back to look towards the bed. In repose, the angular features had softened a little, although still retaining their cleanness of line. Hard to imagine that a mouth which looked so sensitive could be so utterly ruthless. Remembering the feel of it brought a quiver down deep. Considering the circumstances she should be rejecting him on every level, yet her physical responses could hardly be denied. Even if she could trust him to keep his word about not touching her, could she trust herself not to want him to do so?

Shaken, she was forced to acknowledge that mind could not always be relied upon to discipline matter. Luke himself had not been unaffected by that brief but raging contact.

The hollowness in her stomach reminded her that hunger of another kind was still to be satisfied. If he wasn't faking sleep, and it seemed pretty doubtful that he might be, then she had her chance. Once she had eaten she could get down to making concrete plans. What she couldn't afford to do was waste any time about it.

It was cold in the tiny kitchen, a bitterness unrelieved by the austerity of stone sink and peeling paintwork. Of the three cupboards, one contained a couple of saucepans and several pieces of crockery.

Gazing at the padlocked doors of the other two, Gail knew a surge of pure white hot fury. She had to forcibly restrain herself from rushing back into the other room to pound her fists into that carelessly sleeping face. Faced with evidence to the contrary, she had to revise her prior opinion. Not only would he let her go hungry, he would probably enjoy seeing her suffer! The fact that the remedy lay in her own hands was entirely by the way. It was certainly no mitigation.

He had at least left coffee and powdered milk along with the box of matches at the side of the stove. Fingers numb, she lit one of the four burners, shaking the battered kettle to make sure there was water in it before setting it on the flame. How anyone could live this way, even in summer, was beyond her. The place was a wreck!

Waiting for the kettle to boil, she took the opportunity to explore further. Another door at the rear of the kitchen opened into a small porch, which in turn gave access to the primitive toilet. It was clean, and reeked of disinfectant. The biting draught was the worst cross to bear.

The frying-pan Luke had used for the bacon and eggs still lay where he had left it on the sink side, the fat congealed in the bottom. No doubt he had anticipated that she would have seen the light and done the washing-up by the time he surfaced. She might have too, had the thought of getting away not been paramount in her mind. Hunger could be endured; the kind of degradation Luke Richmond had planned for her could not.

A small mirror hung on the wall by the window. Except for the smudges of mascara, she had little make-up left on her face. The edge of a towel dampened with warm water left her feeling rather less tacky, although it didn't do the towel much good. The other one hadn't been used at all. Gail wondered if the same man who stocked the place also did the laundry. There was little enough room in here to hang everything up to dry—although in summer it shouldn't be necessary anyway.

She shook her head impatiently at that point. What on earth did it matter how the washing got done? She wasn't going to be here long enough to be concerned.

With the coffee made, she went back into the other room to sort through the rest of the clothing, this time moving quietly. He had thought of everything, she had to give him that. Apart from spare underwear, there was another pair of trousers and a second sweater, a couple of fine wool shirts, this time taken from Karen's wardrobe, her own flat-heeled casuals, and Karen's sheepskin.

Just as well he'd brought the latter, she reflected dryly, because otherwise she would have been taking his!

The sudden stirring from the bed froze her in her tracks. Luke rolled on to his back, the lifted arm dropping across his chest. Gail waited until his breathing regulated again before daring to relax. The temptation to try removing the car keys from his pocket was great. If she had transport she was home and dry. It took the memory of those well-worn jeans, tight about narrow hips, to deter her. She would never get away with it. No, it was Shanks's pony for her, and the sooner the better. With any luck he would sleep for several hours.

She drank the coffee while she was getting ready. Luke didn't move again. Luckily the bed was out of reach of the first cold shaft of air when she eased open the outer door. Holding her breath, Gail slid through the gap, taking her time in letting the latch down again into position, then standing for a moment with her ear pressed against the wood to listen before finally turning away. So far so good.

The escape added bouyancy to her step until the cold began to get to her. Her feet went first, the thin leather soles affording little protection from the creeping damp of the partially thawed ice that lay in every rut. By the time she came in sight of the little stone bridge she was already soaked, her toes numb.

The cottage was hidden by the curve of the hillside. Stretching to either hand, the narrow road looked as if no motorised vehicle had ever travelled its surface. It said a lot for the Range-Rover's suspension that she hadn't been aware of any real discomfort.

With absolutely no idea of where the road might lead to, she didn't dare take the downhill route which would have been easier, turning her face resolutely in the direction from which they had come that morning. At least it was smoother walking on the worn tarmacadam, although there was enough ice about to make it treacherous in places. Her feet felt like blocks of ice themselves, her finger ends little better. Pockets were no substitute for gloves. Arctic gusts of wind raked her hair back from her face, reddening the skin of her cheeks and making her eyes water. For the first time in her life she began to have some concept of what exposure really meant.

The following hour saw no appreciable change in the lonely landscape. She hadn't yet reached the brow of the hill. She might have turned back had her brain been capable of that much decisiveness after concentrating for so long on simply placing one foot in front of the other. Hunger was a gnawing ache inside her, sapping what resilience she had left. When she heard the engine she couldn't even summon the will to stop and turn.

Luke slid the car to a halt beside her, leaning across

to open the passenger door. 'Fun time over,' he said. 'Get in.'

Gail did so, not caring about anything but the need for warmth. Just to be out of the wind was sheer heaven. 'Believe me,' she said bitterly, 'it's been no fun! I almost froze to death.'

Luke put the vehicle into motion again before answering, easing forward on low revs until the wheels took grip. 'Whose fault was that? If I hadn't woken up when the fire started dying down you'd be out here still.' He gave her a brief, expressionless glance. 'It never occurred to me that you'd be fool enough to try walking out, I have to admit. You don't even know where we are.'

'I didn't even care.' The road flattened out ahead, a level stretch of grass at its side provided turning room. Trying not to beg, she added, 'Why don't you just carry straight on and find somewhere civilised to drop me?'

'It's too soon.' His tone was unrelenting. 'We don't go back to town until the Rivas job has been filled.'

Gail sat huddled into the corner of her seat while he turned the car round, too weary to try again. There was no reasoning with a man of his kind. He had his mind set on a course of action, and he was going to follow it through to the bitter end.

The snow was still holding off when they reached the cottage. Feet unthawed, Gail stumbled and would have fallen when she got out of the car if Luke hadn't been there to swing her upright. It was beautifully warm inside, the fire blazing around the two new logs. The bed was still unfolded. Luke steered her to a seat on the end of it.

'Take off your shoes and stockings,' he said. 'I'll fetch a towel.'

She had managed to comply with both commands by the time he returned, unfastening her suspenders through the material of her trousers, then pulling the stockings by the feet until they slid all the way down. Luke had brought the same towel she had used on her face. He warmed it for a moment or two at the fire before tossing it to her.

'Wrap your toes in that. You're going to find it painful when the circulation starts coming back.'

It was starting already. Gail screwed up her face against the throbbing, determined to allow no single whimper to escape her lips. The growling of her empty stomach was pain of another kind.

'I've put some soup on to heat,' said Luke. 'Only don't take that as a sign of weakness on my part.'

'You don't have to bother,' she retorted scathingly. 'If cooking and kowtowing is part of the exercise then I'll do it, slum conditions or not. How you can bring yourself to live like this at any time is beyond me!'

'They're adequate.' His tone was surprisingly mild. 'Just. Used to belong to a shepherd.'

'You could at least have had it done up.'

'No call. I only use it when I'm feeling in need of total solitude. Working at home is no use when the phone won't stop ringing.'

'Ever tried taking the receiver off?'

'And ignoring the doorbell?' He shook his head. 'Comes a time when the only answer is to cut oneself off for a while. A few weeks up here on my own in the summer sets me up for the rest of the year.'

Gail stared at him curiously, thoughts going off at a tangent. 'Don't you miss certain things?'

'You mean women? I could say the same applies.' He studied her for a moment, attitude difficult to define, then moved over to fish out a pair of warm socks from the clothing still heaped on the chair, dropping them beside her on the bed as he passed. 'I'll get the soup.'

It turned out to be Scotch broth served in a deep bowl along with slices of thick crusty bread. Attacking it, Gail thought she had never tasted anything as good.

'You're not having any?' she asked when the first pangs had been stilled.

Luke had gone to sit in one of the two shabby armchairs, legs stretched before him, arms clasped behind his head. 'I had breakfast,' he reminded her. 'I can wait till lunch.'

Which wouldn't be for another hour or so, Gail realised with a sense of shock, glancing at her watch. So much had happened since their arrival she had somehow imagined it was already late afternoon. She was almost completely thawed out now, and able to think more clearly. Deny it he might, but her attempt to get away had thrown him a little, perhaps even undermined his determination. If she chose her moment carefully there was a chance he might be persuaded to listen to the full story in time to get them out of here before the threatened snowfall.

CHAPTER THREE

LUKE made no comment when, the soup finished, Gail collected his breakfast plate from the table and took both dishes through to the kitchen. The kettle was already on the gas, the water just coming to the boil. She poured the latter into the plastic bowl and refilled the kettle, placing it back on the flame still steadily burning. A cup of coffee might not constitute a very adequate peace-offering, but it was at least a step in the right direction.

There was a bottle of detergent in the cupboard below the sink. Gail squirted some into the bowl, then ran in enough cold water to reduce the heat to a bearable level. Her carefully tended hands and nails were going to suffer, she acknowledged wryly, but there was nothing else for it. Luke was hardly likely to have a pair of rubber gloves around.

The heat was a comfort in the cold kitchen. She lingered longer than necessary over the job. When she did come to dry her hands the varnish was already starting to peel from her nails. Luke hadn't bothered to pick up her handbag, much less her make-up case. The most she could hope for was the loan of a comb, which he would surely not deny her. For the rest, she would just have to grin and bear it.

He was sitting exactly as she had left him when she took the coffee through. To do him credit, there was no self-congratulation in the grey eyes when he took the mug from her with a brief word of thanks. It was almost cosy in the little room, the window panes steamed over from the warmth. Looking at the drab curtains, Gail was sure she had to be the first female to set foot in the place. Convenience aside, no woman could suffer such surroundings without wanting to at least brighten them up.

'Whatever you're planning in that convoluted mind of yours, it won't work,' Luke stated levelly while she was still considering her approach to the subject. 'You've already pulled one stroke too many. Just settle down to the fact that you're not getting out of here until I choose to let you go.'

'Don't you ever let up?' she demanded.

He shrugged. 'You didn't really imagine washing up a few dishes was going to impress me, did you?'

'If I did I was obviously wrong.' Gail looked at him in angry frustration. 'If that snow comes we could be marooned here a whole lot longer than needs be.'

'A chance I'll have to take. I don't have anything pressing on my calendar.'

If she grabbed the fire iron, came the fleeting thought, she could bludgeon him into unconsciousness before he had time to get out of the chair! She knew she was being ridiculous. Violence of that nature needed far more provocation than so far supplied. She tried to view the situation rationally. Having phoned home yesterday she could safely assume there wouldn't be too much concern at that end if she failed to make contact again for a few days. All she had to do was sit tight and hope that fate was on her's and Karen's side. The thought of Luke's reaction if he returned to London to find Karen had stolen a march on him was going to be her only comfort. It would almost make everything worthwhile.

'You'd better open up the cupboards if you want to eat,' she said on a resigned note. 'There's no point in making things any worse than they already are. I'm assuming, since there isn't a fridge, that most of the food is tinned or dried, which is going to limit the menu anyway. I hope you're prepared for a plain diet.'

His smile was singularly lacking in humour. 'I don't doubt your ability to open a tin. Beyond that I don't anticipate very much at all. It won't harm either of us to live on basics for a few days.' He got to his feet, taking a key ring from his pocket. 'I'll show you what there is.'

It wasn't a lot, but it was, Gail supposed, adequate to their needs. There was a small grill mounted above the cooker. She put some bread to toast and opened a tin of beans, studiously ignoring Luke's sardonic expression as he watched her preparations. By tonight she might be bored enough to use a little more imagination; for the moment this was all he merited. He could take it or leave it, she didn't care which.

He accepted his plate without comment when she finally took it through. Still full from the soup, Gail contented herself with a solitary piece of toast scraped with butter, and a mug of tea by way of a change from coffee.

'You didn't give this neighbour of yours a very comprehensive list,' she commented from her seat by the fireside. 'I counted eight tins of beans, the same of stewed steak; the rest are peas, carrots and milk pudding.'

'I didn't give him any list at all,' Luke acknowledged. 'I told him enough for two people for about a week. He probably just doubled up on what he'd buy in for himself.'

'He's a bachelor?'

'A widower, I think. At any rate, he lives alone.' Luke paused, shrugging his shoulders. 'Is it important?'

'It's something to talk about,' she countered. 'We don't have much else.' She was looking at the window where the snow which had started to drift down in occasional flakes some twenty minutes ago was now coming thick and fast with no sign of a lull. Her voice tensed. 'Have you any idea what it's going to be like for two people who despise each other to spend whole days cooped up together in one room?'

'Not pleasant,' he agreed. 'But then I never expected it to be. I'm going to be busy enough myself working on the synopsis of my new book.'

'And what about me?'

'You'll survive. There's a shelf full of reading matter over there if you run out of ideas.'

'I've seen it,' Gail said shortly. 'I'm hardly likely to find much entertainment in back copies of the *Farmer's Weekly*!'

'A parting gift from my predecessor. I tend not to leave anything of mine here over the winter because of the damp, though I might find you a couple of paperbacks in the car. I transported a load to a local jumble sale for my grandmother last weekend. There's always something gets overlooked.'

It was only a little after one o'clock yet because of the worsening weather the room was already growing dim, the firelight casting a cosy glow. With his chair propped on its two rear legs, his heels hooked over the supporting bar of the table and hands wrapped around the mug of hot tea, Luke looked comfortably at ease. Watching the lean, dark profile, Gail felt anything but. Telling herself she hated this man was one thing, teaching her senses to ignore his proximity quite another. She slid her eyes downwards to the tautly muscled thighs, feeling the answering tension in her own; the unleashing of a desire that shamed her. It was almost as if his very animosity was a spur to her emotions.

'I suppose you'll tell me it's irrelevant,' she said a

little too casually, 'if I ask you where your grandmother lives?'

His glance was unfathomable. 'Why the interest?'

'As I said before, just something to talk about.'

'Or someone to complain to when all this is over?' He shook his head. 'You don't really think I'd walk into that trap.'

'I'd never drag in an old lady,' she denied. 'Luke, you have to give me a chance! If I had my handbag here I could prove . . .'

'But you haven't, and I already told you I don't go for that story!' He shoved back his chair with an abruptness that made her shrink involuntarily, leaving the mug on the table to go and pick up his sheepskin. 'I'm going out to the car,' he added on the same short note, shrugging into the coat.

That was it, Gail promised herself fiercely as the door closed behind him. No more appeals, no matter how driven she felt. There was no way he was going to listen.

She took the crockery they had used through to the kitchen while he was out, putting the kettle on the stove and waiting resolutely for it to boil despite the cold. With the few dishes washed and dried there was no further excuse to linger. She went back to the other room to find Luke seated at the table again, a bound wad of A4 paper in front of him. One of the lamps had been lit and stood at his elbow, the soft glow highlighting the droplets of moisture still glistening his hair from the melted snow.

'It might be a good idea if the washing-up was done once a day all together,' he said without looking up from his writing. 'There's a spare cylinder of gas but no point in wasting the stuff.'

Gail made no answer. There was nothing much to say. Three paperback books had been dropped onto

the chair she had occupied previously. She picked
them up, studying the titles without interest as she
took her seat again. No day had ever been as long, no
situation as deadlocked. She wasn't sure how she was
going to stand another hour of it much less a few more
days.

Neither titles nor covers seemed to suggest an
elderly lady's taste in literature. Gail opened the one
depicting a hand holding aloft a bloody dagger on the
front at random, read a few grisly lines and hastily
closed it again, her stomach churning.

'She'll read anything she can lay her hands on,'
Luke remarked, still without glancing up. 'Especially
in winter when she can't get out as much. What she
buys from one jumble sale she sends back to another.
It's her own form of recycling, or so she tells me.'

Gail said softly, 'She sounds quite a character.'

'She is.' He had stopped writing, his tone shorn of
its former harshness. The grey eyes were reminiscent.
'Still lives in the same little house where my father
was born, and doesn't intend moving till they carry
her out in a box—her words not mine. She's in
reasonably good health for her age, but at seventy odd
she needs looking after. I haven't given up hope of
persuading her to go into a nursing home.'

'And rob her of her independence?' The words were
out before she could stop them; she bit her lip as his
eyes swung her way. 'All right, it's not my concern.'

'I was the one who brought the subject up.' His
tone was surprisingly mild. 'You think living alone is a
good thing for any old person these days?'

'Providing they have someone to keep an eye on
them, and I gather you do that.'

'Not as frequently as I'd like.'

'What about the rest of your family then?'

'My parents were divorced when I was eleven.' The

brusqueness was suddenly back again. 'Jeremy, as you know, has other things on his mind. Forget it. I must be mad asking your opinion in the first place!'

Not mad, she thought wryly, just relaxed. For a moment there he had responded to her as a person quite separate from the image he had formed in his mind. He must sense the discordancies yet was simply refusing to take note. Strong-minded or just plain pigheaded? Not that it mattered when the result was the same.

One of the *Tarzan* series by Edgar Rice Burroughs, the second book she opened, proved a little more readable. Gail managed almost three pages before the events of the day combined with the warmth from the fire in eliciting first drowsiness then finally sleep. She awoke with a start when Luke tossed a couple more logs on to the fire, bewildered by the swift transition from half light to full dark outside the window directly facing her.

'It's stopped snowing, if it's of any interest,' he said, straightening to stand with his back to the flames and hands thrust into the pockets of his jeans. 'I'll light the other lamp in a minute.'

No, don't, she wanted to beg. The present glow was comforting. 'How long have I been asleep?' she asked instead.

'A couple of hours.' He watched her sit up and push back the tumbled blonde hair from her face, expression cynical. 'I wouldn't say no to some food if you can make the effort.'

It was an effort to get up from the chair because her foot had gone to sleep. Putting her weight on it, Gail stumbled and would have fallen if Luke hadn't caught her. Held close up against the lean, hard body, she wished fleetingly that things could only be different. She wanted to feel him even closer, to have that mouth of his crushing the breath from her—anything to assuage the ache his very touch created deep inside her. Something kindled in the grey eyes looking down at her. When he bent his head to find her lips it was with sudden fierceness.

The heat from the blazing logs was echoed by that rising inside her. Without thinking about it, she slid both arms around his back until she could feel the hard pressure of his chest against her breasts, lips blindly answering.

He ran his own hands up under her sweater to find the clip of her bra and ease it open, sliding his fingers slowly and tantalisingly across the soft skin beneath her arm until they finally reached the smooth firm swell. Her nipple was already erect, anticipating his caress, the nerve endings raw. She gasped as he rubbed a thumb across it, but came back for more, her body rejecting any last lingering notion of restraint.

It was Luke himself who called the halt, pushing her away from him with suddenly rough hands. 'You'd do just about anything to get yourself out of here, wouldn't you?' he stated harshly. 'Only not with me, because I'm not buying your little tricks!'

Gail took a grip on herself, hating him and wanting him at one and the same moment. 'It was no trick,' she denied with what dignity she could muster. 'I really did fall.'

'And pigs might fly!'

'All right.' She wasn't going to waste her breath on that one either. 'So if you were so sure it was a trick, why let yourself be led by the nose?'

His smile was thin. 'Because like most men I have my moments of weakness, and that was one of them. You've the kind of body it's hard to turn a blind eye to, and you know it. Thrust those breasts of yours against any man the way you did just now and he's going to react. It's a fact of nature. I could get a certain kind of satisfaction from taking you, Karen, but it's not the kind that would give me any lasting pleasure.'

She said bitingly, 'If your own pleasure is all you think about I don't imagine your relationships are very long-lasting anyway!'

'You can console yourself with that thought while you get some food ready,' he responded on a derisive note. 'Just don't take too long about it. I'm hungry.'

If it had been a long day it turned out to be an even longer evening. After a meal of stewed steak, mashed potatoes and tinned peas followed by sago pudding, Luke once again turned to his writing, leaving Gail to the clearing away. She took her time over it, returning to the living room only when the chill of the kitchen became even less bearable than his presence.

For all the notice he took of her she might not have been there at all. Attempting to lose herself in the Tarzan book, she found the print blurring every few minutes as her thoughts veered. She could keep telling herself it was Karen he had rebuffed so contemptuously but it didn't help a great deal when she was the one forced to stand there and take it from him. Who was he to judge her sister so harshly anyway? Karen hadn't forced his brother into having an affair with her; the desire for extra-marital experience must have been there in him. Her only comfort lay in the thought that the moment they did get back to London she could prove she had been telling him the truth all along. At the very least it might teach him not to be quite so ready to prejudge.

She made a hot drink at ten-thirty, setting down the second mug at Luke's elbow with careful restraint.

'Would you mind telling me what the sleeping arrangements are?' she asked shortly. 'I'm tired.'

The glance he directed up at her was distracted, as if his thoughts were still with the plot he was concocting. He seemed to make a conscious effort to drag himself down to earth. 'What did you say?'

'Bed,' she repeated with the same lack of expression. 'I realise you'll probably take this as another proposition, but I want to know where I'm to sleep. Assuming you never intended the two of us to share the one bed, you must have had something in mind.'

There was a visible hardening of resolve in the grey eyes. 'You can take the cushions from the chairs and the sofa back and make a bed on the floor,' he said callously. 'You'll find a couple of spare blankets in the chest over there.' He paused, assessing her reaction. 'Anything else?'

'A comb, if you brought one. Fingers don't make a very adequate substitute unfortunately.'

'No, I can see that.' He got to his feet and went to fetch the small leather case which Gail had imagined would hold a razor. 'I didn't bring you a toothbrush either,' he added. 'I daresay it won't poison us to share.'

She took both items plus a tube of paste from him without a word and headed for the kitchen. There were other things he had forgotten, such as nightwear, but she had no intention of asking for a loan of his pyjama top. Come to think of it, she had seen no sign of those particular garments either when she sorted out the muddle on the chair earlier. No doubt he was one of those hardy creatures who habitually slept in the nude.

There was enough water left in the kettle to provide half a bowlful of luke-warm. Stripping off in the frigid temperature made her gasp. She washed and dried herself hurriedly and slid the sweater back on again while she tackled her hair. The tangles took some getting out. By the time it hung smooth and shining the way it should she was frozen to the marrow and shivering like a leaf.

Back in the other room, she found the cushions already laid out on the floor some feet from the fire, the blankets spread ready. Fresh logs had been fed to the blaze.

'You didn't have to do this,' she said stiffly. 'I could have managed.'

'I'm sure of it.' He sounded indifferent. 'I wanted to see you didn't get too close. We don't have a spark guard.' His glance lingered a moment on her clean-scrubbed face set within the frame of silver-streaked hair, expression revealing little of what was going on in his mind. 'I'll be getting up every couple of hours or so to keep the fire going. No use letting the place get cold again.'

Gail waited until he had gone through to the kitchen himself before stripping off her sweater and slacks and wrapping herself in the blankets. As a bed the arrangement left a lot to be desired, but it was at least better than the bare floor. The wind had risen during the past hour; she could hear it whistling round the chimney. Down here at this level it was draughty, although the heat from the fire was some compensation. She turned on her side with her back to it and huddled the blankets closer about her.

Luke was minus his shirt when he came back from the kitchen, his skin tanned and glowing with a faint healthy sheen. Dark hair covered his chest, tapering off to a fine down where it met the waistband of his jeans.

There was a jingle of metal from the pockets when he took the jeans off. Gail watched him toss them carelessly across the foot of the bed before moving across to the table to turn out the lamp. Barely covered by the black, racing style briefs, his flanks were firm, the muscular structure clearly visible beneath taut stretched skin. The memory of those hard-hewn thighs pressed so closely into hers brought a heated, melting sensation she could scarcely contain. If he knew what he was doing to her it was having no effect on him. He didn't even bother glancing in her direction as he went back to the bed and slid between the sheets.

Moments later his regular breathing told her he was asleep. Gail envied him that ability to turn off both mind and body so readily.

She dozed off herself eventually, wakening with a start when Luke stepped across her to reach the log box.

'Inner time clock,' he said in answer to her unspoken question. 'I can usually set it to within fifteen minutes or so.' He threw another couple of logs on to the fire, this time dusting off his hands together. Only then did he look at her directly, taking in the huddled shape of her body beneath the covering blankets. 'Comfortable?'

'Would it matter if I said no?' she asked shortly. 'You didn't bring me here for my comfort.'

'True,' he agreed. 'Glad you reminded me. I was on the verge of offering to swap.' He took another look at the fire, added, 'That should last a good three hours,' and went back to bed.

Gail waited for sleep to overcome her again, but it had never seemed further away. This whole situation was becoming ludicrous. How Luke could contemplate spending even one more day and night in these conditions was beyond her. It was hardly necessary anyway. The fact that Karen Greer had been unavailable today would have put paid to her chances where the Rivas job was concerned. With so little time in which to find their replacement and so many names to choose from, they were hardly going to wait around for one girl to turn up. Satisfying though Karen's timely return would have been, it was hardly likely to have happened. Fate didn't move in such fortuitous ways.

Turning restlessly on to her side, she lay gazing at the bed with its recumbent occupant, wishing she could follow his example in blotting out the whole situation. Attracted to him she might be in spite of herself, but that in no way altered anything. If there was some way of turning the tables on him she would seize it with both hands!

It was only then that she recalled the clink of metal when he had tossed his jeans down on the bed. The car keys, of course! Trying to walk out this morning had been a mere gesture, and they had both known it, but if she could get away with the car he would be stranded.

She slid cautiously out from under the blankets, shivering a little as she moved away from the immediate circle of heat but too intent on achieving her aim to let the cold deter her. First secure the keys, then she could think about getting dressed. If Luke did happen to waken while she was doing it, she could always make the excuse that she needed to visit the lean-to. He would hardly expect her to brave that place in bra and pants.

The first pocket she tried contained only loose change. She held her breath at the unavoidable sounds she made in lifting the jeans to get at the other pocket, but there was no movement from the bed. The breath came out again on a faint sigh of triumph as her groping fingers closed on their quarry. For a shattering moment there it had occurred to her that he might have secured the car keys elsewhere at some time during the day. So far so good. She had never driven a Range-Rover before but one vehicle was much the same as another when it came to getting it started. All she had to do was drive until she came on some signpost to somewhere, then follow her nose. There may even be a map if she was lucky.

The sudden flinging back of the covers and forward dive took her totally by surprise, freezing her in the very act of turning away. Next moment she was flat on her face with the breath driven from her as Luke dragged her bodily across the bed towards him. One hand clamped the back of her neck, holding her down, while the other ruthlessly extracted the keys from her grasp, tossing them on to the bedside cupboard with ominous force. Only then did he roll her over to straddle her, both hands clamping her shoulders to the mattress. The flickering, leaping light from the fire gave the lean features a devilish cast.

'I've been waiting for you to try pulling some stunt like that one,' he said with derision. 'You really thought you'd got away with it, didn't you?'

The realisation that he had been lying there faking sleep all the time she had been searching his pockets snapped whatever control Gail had left. That the vicious upthrust of her knee failed to connect with its target area was due only to Luke's speed of reaction, thudding instead into the muscle of his inner thigh and drawing a muffled grunt. For a long moment he was still, absorbing the pain, then anger came leaping into his eyes, thinning his lips to a merciless line.

'If it's rough play you like I can accommodate you,' he gritted.

Gail was helpless to stop him removing her scanty clothing. There was no gentleness in the hands he ran over her body; his touch was meant to humiliate not incite. A quiver ran through her when he drew back to study her with that same hard appraisal, but she refused to turn her face away, eyes blazing defiance. Let him look; she had nothing to be ashamed of!

She sensed the moment at which the anger in him began to change character, but it wasn't until he let out his breath on a long drawn sigh and lowered his body slowly into contact with her again that she knew for certain what was in his mind.

'Damn you!' he said thickly. 'Damn you, damn you, damn you!'

There was no resisting that mouth of his. After a moment or two there was no longer even the desire to resist it. Her fingers fluttered over his back, stroking, urging, burying themselves in the thick dark hair of his head as he lowered his seeking lips to her breast. The touch of his tongue triggered off waves of sensuous pleasure, arching her back in compulsive response. She pressed her own lips to his flesh, tasting the salt on his skin, scenting the erotic male odour, feeling the unrestricted, potent weight of him pressuring open her thighs.

At the back of her mind the small voice of reason was desperately trying to make itself heard, telling her she would regret this, but she turned a deaf ear. It was too late for regrets, too late for anything except what was happening to her now this very minute because he was right there inside her, an integral part of her, moving to a rhythm that built with each pulse beat to a point where there was only one release.

It was necessary to start coming down to earth some time, Gail knew, yet in those following fleeting moments when she still held the dark head cradled against her breast she found herself wishing they could just go on being together. Making love was an art she had only just begun to learn, and the only teacher she wanted was this man with her. What had happened between them just now was as nothing compared with what could; every sense in her told that much. It had been over so quickly – too quickly. Hardly surprising considering the circumstances, she supposed. Luke had taken her against his better instincts, hating his weakness even as he indulged it.

She made no attempt to hold him when he lifted up away from her. There was no point in trying to prolong the inevitable. He sat on the bed edge for a moment with his back to her before reaching out a suddenly resolute hand for his clothes.

'Get dressed,' he said harshly without turning his head towards her. 'We'll leave at first light.'

Whatever she had been expecting it wasn't that. Voice low, she said, 'You're taking me back?'

'That's the sum of it.' He stood up to pull on jeans and sweater, only then sparing her a glance. 'You won, didn't you. I couldn't even keep my hands off you for twenty-four hours! I suppose I should find some consolation in knowing I'm not the first catch you've landed, and I sure as hell won't be the last. You're a living man trap, Karen. Give credit where credit's due. Only this is going to be one who got away!'

'It wasn't like that,' she said, still unable to bring herself to move. Her voice sounded thick and tight. 'You're blaming me for inciting you, Luke, but you were the one who started it. You could have taken the keys away from me without pulling me into bed with you.'

'Think I don't know it?' He went over to pick up her sweater and cords, tossing them at her with a heavy hand. 'I said get dressed!'

She obeyed because there wasn't much else she could do, pulling on the garments with hands that felt nerveless. 'What about the Rivas job?' she asked. 'Aren't you afraid it might still be open?'

'It's a chance I'll take.' He was lighting the lamp, his every movement rigidly controlled. 'I was a fool bringing you here in the first place. You started getting to me the minute we met, and you knew it. It was playing right into your hands.'

'I can't be held responsible because you find it so hard to say no to yourself,' she retorted bitterly. 'You're not the only one with regrets.'

He looked at her then, a long hard glance. 'What's one more in the long run? Can you even remember the first man you went to bed with?'

She swallowed hard, too well aware of the futility in reiteration. 'The trouble with men like you,' she said instead, 'is you still think you should hold a monopoly on sexual experience. You treat women casually because that's all they mean to you, yet you're the first to complain when the attitude rubs off. Did you ever have even one really lasting relationship in *your* life, Luke?'

'If I did,' he said, 'you'd hardly be the one I'd tell about it.' His eyes were steely. 'You're trying to make out Jeremy only wanted sex too?'

That 'too' hurt but she wasn't about to let him know it. She shrugged. 'Basically.'

'So why should he leave his family?'

'Perhaps because he's too immature to realise what's really important in life. Perhaps because his wife didn't quite satisfy his oh so vital masculine needs! Maybe with two young children to occupy her time and attention she neglected to succour his ego. I can imagine any brother of yours finding that hard to take!' The pause held deliberation. 'I don't somehow think he'd be all that delighted to find out what you've been up to this last couple of days either.'

Luke's face was a mask. 'You're thinking of telling him?'

The fire went out of her suddenly, leaving her weary and deflated. 'No, I'm not thinking of telling him. So far as I'm concerned, the sooner I'm done with the whole Richmond clan, the better! Just get me back to London, that's all I ask.'

'I intend to. Just as soon as it's light enough to travel.' He was moving as he spoke, the words jerked from his lips. 'I'll make a drink.'

Left alone, Gail stood for a long moment gazing into space before forcing herself to pick up the blankets from the floor in front of the fire and start folding them. With the cushions replaced on the two chairs, she turned her attention to the bed, stripping it down to the bare mattress and doubling the base back into place beneath the seat. It was some relief to get it out of the way, though nothing could rid her of the images crowding her mind. Some day she would find another man who could bring her alive the same way Luke had done in those emotive moments, and really mean something by it. It might not be soon but it was going to be worth waiting for.

CHAPTER FOUR

WINTER dusk had fallen by the time they reached London after hold-ups *en route* due to weather conditions. Luke carried Gail's things up to the flat, dumping the load down on the floor with scant ceremony.

'You'll excuse me if I don't hang around,' he said unemotionally. 'I shan't be bothering you again, in any sense.'

Gail stayed where she was gazing at the door for several minutes after it had closed behind him, her own emotions far from equable. These past few hours had been a nightmare in more ways than one. Luke had scarcely spoken a word during the whole long drive, but the enmity radiating from him had been unmistakable. It was difficult to accept that only this morning she had lain in his arms and felt the intimate intrusion of his body, yet the memory was still too clear and emotive to be put aside. The knowledge that she would not be seeing him again formed a cold hard knot at the centre of her being.

Eventually she forced herself to move, lifting the cover on the mailbox attached to the back of the door-slot to extract the two envelopes contained within. One was a circular, the other an obvious bill. Dispiritedly she put both down on the lobby table before going to sort out the clothing Luke had tossed down. Karen had no right to leave her suspended this way, yet what could she do about it when she didn't even have an address at which to contact her? There was always the alternative of simply walking out on the situation, of course, but could she bring herself to do it? Karen might return at any time. She would just have to hope that it would be soon. Living the lie was going to be even harder now.

The telephone answering machine had a light on, indicating a message or messages to be relayed. Gail switched it on after returning from the bedroom, standing to listen with scant interest to the disembodied voice. There were three messages in all, each successive one more urgently phrased. 'Where on earth are you?' came the final frantic plea from an agent obviously at her wits' end. 'They won't extend the option beyond eight o'clock tonight, so for God's sake contact me the minute you get in! I'll be at the office.'

The Rivas contract, was Gail's first thought. It had to be the Rivas contract! Little else could have disturbed Norah Bates' equanimity to such a degree. The problem was did eight o'clock tonight refer to today or yesterday? There was no way of telling from the machine itself.

Fingers trembling a little, she dialled the memorised number, listening with fast-beating heart to the ringing tone at the far end of the line. The other receiver was snatched up before the second tone was completed. 'Karen?' came the urgent query. 'Is that you?'

'Yes.' Her jaw was so tense, Gail could scarcely force the acknowledgment out. 'What is it, Norah?'

'Rivas. They want you for *Promise*! We've less than three hours to clinch it. Where the hell have you been the last two days?'

'I-I took a break.' There was little else Gail could find to say. 'Sorry about this morning.'

'Never mind that now. The main thing is you're back. Just get yourself over here in the next hour.

I'm going to ring Paul Denham right now and tell him you're available.' The tone was crisp and not a little edged. 'Just thank your lucky stars I managed to persuade him to give me some extra time or you'd be looking for another agency. This is one job we'd hate to have lost!'

Gail could imagine. Replacing the receiver, she stood for a bare moment trying to collect herself together. So Luke had failed. He wasn't going to like that either. Not that there was very much he could do about it now. They wanted her enough to hold on for almost two whole days. No, not her, Karen, she reminded herself wryly. And there lay the real problem. The job included television commercial work, of which she had absolutely no experience. Could she possibly cope well enough to satisfy those who were going to be sinking so much advertising capital into this campaign?

One thing was certain, she acknowledged ruefully a moment later, she was unlikely to find out until she tried it. Like it or not, nerves had to be conquered and courage found. The Agency would never forgive her if she made a mess of such an opportunity.

She was ready in less than thirty minutes, the beige wool jumpsuit and toning gilet complemented by calf-high boots and Karen's sheepskin. With her hair twisted up under the matching hat and her face highlighted by a skillfully applied make-up, she hoped her appearance would impress this Paul Denham sufficiently to make him forget how long he had been kept waiting. This was Karen's big chance too; she couldn't afford to fluff a single line.

The Agency offices were on Jermyn Street. As might be anticipated at this hour of the evening, the outer doors were locked. Gail rang the bell, waiting two or three minutes for Norah to descend from the first floor to open up for her.

'You've got some explaining to do,' stated the older woman briefly as she locked up again before leading the way upstairs. 'I've been going frantic trying to trace your whereabouts!'

'I can guess,' Gail acknowledged wryly. 'It's just . . .'

'Save it for later. Right now there's only one person you have to satisfy, and that's Denham. He's capable of doing a turn-round even now if he thinks they made a mistake.'

Gail kept her gaze straight ahead, concentrating on the turn of the stair. 'I don't think I ever met him before.'

'It's doubtful,' Norah agreed dryly. 'You haven't been moving on that level.'

'What made them choose me at all?' Gail asked curiously. 'I mean, there must be dozens they could have used with far more experience.'

'Such modesty!' The woman gave her an odd glance. 'Is this the same girl who told me only the other week that she had it in her to go right to the top?'

'Did I say that?' Gail kept her voice deliberately light. 'It must have been one of my more self-confident days. I fluctuate rather a lot.'

'So I've been noticing—though only this past couple of weeks or so.' This time the glance was sardonic. 'If it's a man you'd better forget him. You're going to be too busy to even think about sex, much less practice it!'

Gail bit her tongue, conscious that the comment was probable based on actual knowledge rather than guesswork. Her sister's reputation left a whole lot to be desired, and there was little she could do to repute it. She would gladly relinquish all claim to fame and fortune if only Karen would get herself back home.

Norah hadn't answered her question, and there was no time to repeat it because the other was already opening her office door, her face breaking into a smile as she looked across at the man standing at the uncurtained window.

'Here she is at last! Worth waiting for, wouldn't you say?'

'Let's hope so,' came the smooth reply. 'I laid my neck on the line for you, Norah. You owe me one.'

'I'll remember.' Her equilibrium remained unruffled. 'Take your coat off, honey. Let Paul see what he's buying.'

The Rivas representative was a man of medium height and stocky build, his features square set beneath the dark brown hair. About forty, Gail guessed, and nobody's fool. Blue eyes regarded her with steady assessment.

'Good figure,' he commented when the sheepskin had been removed. 'Done any underwear?'

'Not lately,' Gail replied, playing safe.

'Swimwear,' Norah supplied. 'But her face wasn't used. Nobody's going to recognise the boobs.' She gave a small hard smile. 'You've done your homework already on this one, Denham. Don't try to kid me.'

'Sure.' He was looking at Gail, the expression in his eyes discomfiting. 'You're going to find your personal life a mite curtailed while you're under contract to us. Having a *femme fatale* promote *Promise* won't do the image any harm, just providing it's kept within certain bounds. What we don't need is any scandal. That means no home-breaking for starters.'

Gail flushed, biting her lip. The longing to tell the two of them what they could do with their precious job was strong, but loyalty was stronger. If Karen

would only come home they could do the swap with
no one any the wiser. She herself would be grateful to
retire to her own home for a while in order to review
her plans. There were other ways she could make a
new start.

'I'll bear it in mind,' she said, trying not to sound
too sarcastic. 'You're in charge.'

'That's right.' His smile was sudden and attractive.
'I think we're going to get along just fine.'

'You're well suited,' Norah advised, sounding
tongue-in-cheek. Expression bland, she picked up a
paper from her desk. 'So let's get down to the nitty-
gritty, shall we?'

As Paul had stated, Gail found little time during the
days following to think about anything but the actual
job in hand. Filming a two-minute commercial proved
to be even less of a sinecure than she had anticipated,
with take after take discarded in the search for that
combination of expression, gesture and spoken word
which would impel women all over Britain to rush out
and snap up the product that was going to change
their whole lives for the better. They did a series of
three to start, which together with magazine and
billboard coverage formed the basis of the initial
campaign. If successful, there would be other
campaigns to follow, though Gail refused to think
about that distant future. Right now she had all she
could cope with just playing her part.

The first time Paul Denham asked her out to dinner
she refused point blank without trying to wrap it up,
still smarting on Karen's behalf for the things he had
said, deserved though they might be. He accepted the
refusal without argument, but it didn't stop him
asking. Had Gail found him personally unappealing
there would have been no problem, yet there was no

question that beneath that no-nonsense exterior lurked a man of considerable charm when he cared to extend himself.

'You're wasting your time,' she said bluntly to him on the third occasion after a hard day's shooting. 'If it's an easy lay you want you'd better try somewhere else!'

'The invitation was to dinner,' he returned, quite unperturbed. 'Anything else would be in the lap of the Gods. Okay, so I got across you the first time we met. I apologise for not waiting to form my own opinion. So far as I'm personally concerned, what you do in your own time is your own affair. I never saw any reason why women shouldn't feel the same freedom to indulge an instinct.' He put a hand on her arm as she made to turn away, drawing her back to face him. The blue eyes were steady. 'Just one thing I want to make clear. There'd be no coercion to get you into bed. Too much depends on you to risk alienating you in any fashion. I've an odd feeling you wouldn't exactly be sorry if the whole thing fell through before it got off the ground.'

He was too perceptive by half, Gail reflected, holding his gaze with an effort. Disarming too in his ready acknowledgment of fault. She found her lips widening into an involuntary smile. Paul had never known Karen herself on any personal basis so there was little danger of his recognising the basic differences. The fact that eventually there may come a time when he would be in a position to draw comparisons she chose to ignore. Paul was as different from Luke as chalk from cheese, his straightforward approach a tonic in itself. One would know exactly where one stood with a man of his calibre.

'All right,' she said, 'you talked me into it.'

That was the start of a relationship which over the

coming days was to prove a great comfort. True to his word, Paul made no attempt to step out of line, leaving her to set the pace. In his company she was able to relax and be herself, drawing him out to talk in a manner she fancied he rarely did. He was thirty-nine years old, and had been with Rivas for the last five of them. Parted from his wife for three years, he admitted that divorce was, as yet, a step he couldn't bring himself to take.

'We were married when we were both in our early twenties,' he said on one occasion. 'It was too soon to know what we wanted out of life. A baby might have made a difference, but Maureen couldn't conceive. Maybe subconsciously she was fighting the whole idea of being tied down to that extent. She's in the same line of business working in Canada at the moment. One of these days we're going to have to get round to sorting ourselves out.'

'I suppose there's no real urgency,' Gail acknowledged. 'Not until one of you needs the freedom.' She studied him a moment across the restaurant table, warming to his rugged looks. 'You know, you're nothing like my image of a promotions man. If I had to guess, I'd put you down for a property tycoon!'

'Flattery,' he said on an equally light note, 'will get you everywhere. Why property in particular?'

Gail lifted her shoulders laughingly. 'It sounds impressive, and you look impressive. You always wear such superbly tailored suits.'

'I have to,' he said. 'I'm too thickset to get away with anything but. Charlie told me that first time we met.'

'Charlie?' Gail queried, and received a surprised glance.

'Charlene Rivers—president of Rivas. Everybody in the business knows her as Charlie. She's the one who picked you out of the line-up the morning we lost Bailey. She thought you had a presence the other girls didn't. She's also the reason we gave Norah the extra time to get hold of you, although I wasn't letting her know that. Personally, I'd have gone with the second choice.' He smiled a little. 'Not that I wouldn't have been sorry to have missed you. Charlie was right on all counts. As she said at the time, whoever it was said there was no smoke without fire never came camping with her!'

Gail was only half-listening, her mind still several sentences back. 'You mean a photographic line-up?'

'Obviously. You did a session for Silk shampoo last week with Tim Jackson. We wanted to keep the agencies out of it until we made our choice, so we had him supply a couple of shots in your case.'

They had chosen her, not Karen, she realised dazedly. They thought *she* had presence!

'Something wrong?' asked Paul on a curious note. 'You look as if somebody just pole-axed you.'

Gail shook herself mentally, her smile wide and bright. 'Not a thing. Thank Charlie for me when you see her, will you?'

'You can do it yourself come the weekend,' he said. 'She wants you to come down to the house with me. There'll be a party of us; there always is. Charlie likes having people round her.'

'How old is she?'

'Seventy going on fifty. She has enough energy for three!' He paused, waiting, head on one side. 'You are going to come, I hope?'

Gail laughed. 'As if I could refuse, even if I wanted to! I'll look forward to meeting her. Where is it, by the way?'

'Dorset. Bockhampton. Thomas Hardy was born there. Not that Charlie's planning on leaving a lesser impression.' Paul lifted a hand to the waiter. 'Time I took you home. You've another tough day ahead.'

That night, as on others before it, he kissed her goodnight at her door. Gail found the experience enjoyable if not especially stirring. After Luke it was going to take a lot to reach her, she thought ruefully when she was alone again. It was the first time in days she had allowed her mind to dwell on that individual. Thinking about him at all was a pointless exercise when it was unlikely they would ever even meet again.

There was still no word from Karen by the weekend. Gail put the problem firmly to the back of her mind, determined to enjoy this brief respite. Had she ever believed there was any glamour attached to filming, this past week had taught her better, although she couldn't say she had hated the work either. Knowing she had been chosen on the strength of her own qualities was all the boost her spirits needed when the going got hard. Relinquishing that position might not be so easy when the time came.

Paul drove her down to the house in a company Daimler, an unfamiliar and oddly unimpressive figure in tweeds. Clad in its winter garb, the countryside held little of Hardy's rich colour, yet the feeling was there. Villages came and went, each one different in character. Passing through Lower Bockhampton, they turned away from the upper hamlet to take a private roadway through a large estate rising towards the heath. Gail exclaimed in admiration at her first sight of the beautifully restored Elizabethan manor framed by tall bare elms which mercifully seemed to have escaped the devastation wrought among their kin.

'Charlie bought the place five years ago when it was virtually falling down,' said Paul as they drew up before the great oak doors. 'She calls it her monument.

I daresay it will still be here when we're all of us long gone.' His nod indicated the three cars parked along the front of the house. 'Seems we're not the only ones invited for lunch. The Porsche belongs to one of Charlie's grandsons. If I know Luke he'll have some woman in tow.' He got out of the car, bending to peer back in at her when she failed to move, a quizzical smile touching his lips. 'Waiting for me to play the gentleman?'

Gail forced nerveless limbs into movement, finding some suitably light quip in reply. Of course it wasn't him, she reassured herself. It was hardly that unusual a name. Hadn't he described his grandmother as still living in the same little house where his father had been born? This could hardly be that. Yes, came the answering thought, but a man could have more than one grandparent still living, and in differing circumstances at that. Heart sinking, she recalled that very first conversation the night Luke Prentis had abducted her from the flat. Only on the fringe, he had said when she had asked him if he was involved in advertising. If Charlene Rivers really was his grandmother it would explain how he had come to hear about Cassie Bailey's accident before the media had even got hold of it. It would explain a whole lot.

The grand entrance hall rose the full height of the house, surrounded on three sides by a galleried landing. Suits of armour stood to eternal attention at intervals along both side walls, while down the centre of the stone-flagged floor ran a long refectory table in solid oak. The lovely flower arrangement in the centre of the latter brought light and warmth into the place.

Voices came from within partially opened double doors on the far side of the hall, but the uniformed maid who had admitted them made no attempt to lead them hither, making instead for the imposing sweep of staircase. They had rooms set opposite across a corridor, the two of them superbly furnished in period with four-poster beds and velvet drapes.

'Lunch is in half an hour,' the maid informed them before leaving. 'Madam will be pleased to see you in the drawing room for drinks after you freshen up from your journey.'

Still standing in the doorway of her own room, Gail looked across at Paul and grinned. 'It sounds like a command appearance.'

'It is,' he agreed. 'You're her showpiece for the weekend. Don't be fooled by the benevolent approach when you meet her. There's little of the sweet old lady about our Charlie.'

'You make her sound a regular ogress.' Casually, she added, 'This grandson of hers, is he in advertising too?'

'Only as a Company shareholder these days. He's made another fortune writing thrillers. You've probably heard of Luke Prentis?'

'Yes, of course.' Her voice sounded odd; she made an effort to control it. The smile she gave him was over-bright. 'See you in ten minutes.'

So her fears had not been unfounded, she thought with trepidation when the door was safely closed. Well, at least forewarned was forearmed, although quite how she was going to handle the situation she wasn't sure.

It was then, gazing unseeingly at the painting on the far wall that the idea came to her, tensing the muscles of her stomach in sudden nervous excitement. Luke believed she was really Karen, didn't he? So all right, this time there would be no argument from her. If she could carry off the plan even now taking shape in her mind she would have the most wonderful revenge anyone could ever hope for. And she would carry it off. The opportunity was just too good to pass up.

She had changed into one of Karen's most eye-catching dresses by the time Paul tapped on her door. Cling-pleated from neck to hem in oblique stripes of beiges and browns, it skimmed her figure with subtle emphasis. Paul nodded approvingly when she opened the door to him.

'That should knock their eyes out okay! Charlie will be delighted. She likes making an entrance herself.'

'You don't think it's too much for lunchtime?' Gail asked, still not too sure of herself, and took immediate reassurance from the unhesitating shake of his head.

'You're a model, not a nonentity. You'll be expected to look the part.' Blue eyes considered her thoughtfully for a moment. 'You know, you have me confused. Sometimes it's almost as if you're two different people.'

Gail's heart jerked then steadied again. 'Feminine perversity,' she came back glibly. 'Let's go on down.'

At first glance the large and lovely drawing room seemed full of people, all of whom stopped talking in order to view the newcomers as they stepped through the doors. Luke was over by one of the windows with an auburn-haired woman; that much Gail was able to take in before Charlene Rivers came stepping nimbly across to greet the two of them, face lit by a welcoming smile.

'So glad you could make it, dears,' she said, as if they had either of them had a choice. 'Paul, you know everybody here so you won't mind if I take Karen away from you.' The eyes which had never left Gail's face might be faded a little from their original blue-grey, but they had retained all their shrewdness and perspicacity. 'You're even lovelier than your photo-graphs—and that dress is a dream!'

Gail smiled back as she murmured the appropriate response, aware of Luke's regard and the dampness of her palms. Considering the fact that his ruse to deprive her of this very job had failed to work out, she was surprised that he should be here at all. Unless he hadn't known she was invited. She took care not to look in his direction as Charlene began introducing other members of the party, steeling herself for the moment when the inevitable must happen. Her initial intention had been to greet him as a total stranger, not only in words but in every visible sense. Only when they finally came face to face did instinct supply a more subtle approach, summoning a small knowing smile to her lips as she lifted bland eyes to the strong features.

'We never met before but I've *heard* so much about you,' she said with faint but unmistakable emphasis. 'I've read all your books.'

The fingers briefly clasping hers had a iron hardness that matched the line of his mouth. 'Hope you enjoyed them.'

'Oh, I did! And having met you, I can see where your heroes might be just a bit of a self-extension.' She was enjoying herself now, relishing the faint uncertainty in his eyes. She had told him several times that she had a twin sister. Perhaps he was finally beginning to suspect that she might have been telling the truth. This weekend was going to be more fun than she had anticipated. Just let him wait!

The red-head had already been introduced as Lorraine Dedbury. From the way she was sticking so close to Luke, Gail guessed she was his guest for the weekend. Beautiful but hard as nails, was her mental summing up. They suited one another admirably.

She found herself seated right across from him at the lunch table, making it difficult to relax even for a moment. On several occasions she caught him watching her, giving him the same bland little smile which hinted at secret amusement. There was going to come a time when he would seek her out in private and demand a reckoning, there was nothing surer than that. She had to be ready for him, careful to say nothing that might give her away. He was going to pay and pay dearly for everything he had done to her.

Charlene watched her too, although less obviously. Seated at the head of the long polished table, she looked positively regal, her head of silver white hair smoothed into a perfect chignon. The lines on her face could not detract from the superb bone-structure. In her heyday, Gail reflected, she must have been truly lovely. Slender as a reed, she looked as good as many a woman half her age in the classic jersey dress the same colour as her eyes. From what little she knew, it seemed that Luke's mother might have married out of her class. Luke had told her his parents had been divorced but not whether they were still alive. Perhaps like hers they had both of them married again.

'You're looking very pensive,' murmured Paul, breaking in on her thoughts. 'Something worrying you?'

Luke was listening; Gail could almost feel him tuning in. 'Nothing at all,' she responded brightly. 'I just drifted off for a moment. The sun's come out. Do you feel like a walk in the grounds after lunch?'

'Sorry,' he said regretfully. 'Charlie wants to see me on business. Maybe later.'

'It doesn't matter,' she hastened to assure him. 'I can go on my own. It's too nice an afternoon to waste indoors.'

'You're telling me.' He laughed and shrugged. 'It goes with the job. I'm not complaining. There's always tonight.'

There was something in the way he said it that made her glance at him a little sharply, wondering if the proximity of their rooms had been arranged. Because he had so far made no attempt to further their relationship didn't necessarily mean that he had no intention. He was attracted to her, that much he had made plain. There was no reading anything from his expression. Neither, she had to admit, was there any point in considering her actions until she was faced with the problem. She liked Paul a lot, but she didn't want an affair with him. She didn't want an affair with anybody.

The February sunshine might look bright but she was well aware that it was unlikely to have any real warmth. Before setting out on her exploration of the grounds once Paul had vanished into some inner sanctum with Charlene, she went back upstairs and changed again into the slacks and sweater in which she had travelled, pulling on a pair of brogues and the sheepskin jacket. From the sound of it, the rest of the party had retired once more to the drawing room by the time she got downstairs. By dint of trial and error, she eventually found a corridor which gave access to a side door, slipping out into the cold but stimulating air with a sense of freedom.

The grounds were extensive, with only the areas immediately surrounding the house itself cultivated to a degree. There was a swimming pool at the rear—empty at present, of course—and a tennis court beyond that. Cutting through the edge of a small copse, Gail was delighted and intrigued to find a real maze, its hedges neatly trimmed to a height far above her head.

She spent half an hour threading her way to the centre, sinking down on the stone seat surrounding the sundial with a sense of achievement and a laugh at the faint superstition that had made her fancy footsteps following her once or twice. If finding her way out again was going to take as long she had better not linger or they would be sending out search parties. Already the winter afternoon was drawing in, the sun hidden behind gathering cloud. She shivered a little despite the enveloping coat, then felt her heart leap almost into her throat as a tall dark figure appeared in the narrow walkway.

'It's as good a place as any,' Luke said grimly. 'At least we're unlikely to be interrupted.' He stayed where he was, familiar yet unfamiliar in the short camel overcoat. 'Now supposing you tell me what game we're supposed to be playing?'

Gail took a hold on herself. This moment had had to come sooner or later. What difference did it make? She made her tone deliberately light and mocking.

'No game, Mr Prentis—or may I call you Luke? After all Gail told me about you, I don't feel we need stand on any ceremony!'

He was very still, expression unnerving. 'Gail?' he queried.

'My sister. My *twin* sister.' She relished the look in his eyes. 'You just wouldn't be convinced, would you?'

'You're lying again.' The statement was harsh. 'You're the same girl I . . .'

'The same girl you raped?' she broke in softly, watching his face change. 'Am I really? You're quite sure about that?'

The silence stretched between them, the seconds ticking by inexorably. When he spoke again it was in a tone that made her shiver inwardly. 'Raped?'

'You're trying to say that isn't what happened?'

'I'm not trying to say anything,' he clipped. 'You asked for everything you got!'

'Not me,' she insisted without raising her voice. 'My sister. And I'm sure she didn't. Not Gail. She told me how you dragged her on to that bed, how you tore off her clothes, how you forced her to do what you wanted. She told me everything. Who else did she have to talk to?'

The grey eyes were narrowed, seeking to penetrate her defences. Gail met his gaze squarely, determined not to give way. She was in too deep now anyway. There could be no going back. She didn't want to go back.

'If you'd waited a couple of minutes the night you brought her back to the flat you'd have met me then,' she went on. 'I got in half an hour before you did. I was in the kitchen making some coffee when you arrived. It took me quite some time to drag the story out of her.' She studied him, sensing his change of attitude. It hardly needed the distracted run of one lean hand through his hair to convince her that she was winning this initial battle. 'Naturally, I took over my own life again right away,' she added, pressing home her advantage. 'I was obviously meant to get this contract.'

'So where is she now?' The question was growled.

'Back home, where else? After what you did to her she needed time to recover.'

'I did nothing she didn't want too!' He paused there, catching his lower lip between his teeth. 'If I had to resort to rape I'd give up the game altogether!'

'Oh, I can imagine.' She let her eyes drift slowly and insinuatingly down the length of his body, the way Karen herself might well have done in similar circumstances. 'Perhaps Gail just wasn't experienced enough to recognise the difference between passion and violation. We were parted when we were children, you see. She grew up in a provincial town. I daresay the boys she knows back home don't have quite the same way with them. I only hope you haven't turned her off the whole idea of sex. It sometimes . . .'

'Cut it out!' He said it softly enough but with a very real threat behind the words. 'I might have made one mistake, but I know genuine response when I feel it. Your sister is no wilting violet.'

'I'll tell her when I see her again. I doubt if she'll be flattered.' Gail pushed herself to her feet, drawing the sheepskin closer up about her neck. 'I'd better be getting back or Paul will think I've got lost. Your grandmother should be through with him by now, wouldn't you say?'

'Probably.' He made no attempt to move, effectively blocking her passage. 'Is he your latest?'

'He's a friend,' she said steadily. 'A very good friend. I don't owe you any confidences, Luke. I never owed you anything.'

'What about Jerry?'

'What about him? Gail did me a favour giving him the push. I couldn't bring myself to tell him to go.' Her voice hardened a fraction. 'The trouble with that brother of yours is he never grew up. Fighting his battles for him won't help him do it.'

The grey eyes had narrowed again. 'This sister of yours used pretty much the same words.'

'Which just goes to prove we see things the same way.' She would have to watch her step, Gail reflected dryly, or she was going to fall flat on her face. 'Are you going to let me pass?'

His mouth twisted. 'Why not? I'll even show you the way back. It's the least I can do under the circumstances.'

Looking back on the moment afterwards, Gail knew she should have anticipated the grab he made for her as she made to pass him. As it was, she had bare seconds to steel herself against the demanding pressure of his lips, the warmth of his hands sliding under her coat. Held against that lean body, she put everything she knew into remaining perfectly still, fighting the urges rising so swiftly and sharply in her. Her mouth felt numb when he finally let her go, but she managed to meet his eyes without a flicker.

'Not bad,' she said, 'but I've known better. Did you settle any last doubts?'

'You could say that.' He was ignoring the sneer. 'That's one way the two of you differ.'

'You mean you like to believe we do. If you knew the way Gail really feels about you you wouldn't be so complacent. She still carries the bruises.'

'I think you've said just about enough,' came the hard response. 'If you don't want to stay out here in the dark just keep your mouth closed. Okay?'

She made a mute gesture, knowing full well that such obedience to the letter would rile him even more. She had won the day, yet she could find little satisfaction in the thought. His attraction was too real to be denied. That he wouldn't be touching her again was more than apparent. What she must do now was teach herself not to care.

CHAPTER FIVE

PAUL was just setting out to look for her when they got back to the house. He watched the two of them coming across the grass without expression, unbuttoning his heavy jacket again.

'Enjoy your walk?' he asked as they reached the doorway. 'Lorraine was looking for you, Luke.'

'I daresay.' The other sounded brusque. 'Where's Charlie?'

'With the others. She was worried about Karen.' Blue eyes studied her face, missing nothing. 'You look as if you need a drink. There's tea in the drawing room—or would you rather have something stronger?'

'What I'd really like is a warm bath,' she acknowledged, passing by him. 'Do you think Mrs Rivers will mind if I give tea a miss?'

'Nobody calls my grandmother anything but Charlie,' Luke put in, tossing his coat across a nearby chair. 'You'd better do the same. I'll make your excuses for you if you like.'

'Thanks.' She kept her own tone just as short. 'I'll see you later, Paul.'

He moved after her, catching her up at the foot of the staircase, a question in his eyes. 'Did something happen out there?'

'You mean with Luke?' Gail shrugged and lifted her eyebrows, realising that Paul would not be easily deceived. 'Nothing I couldn't handle. Unlike his grandmother, he takes hearsay as gospel!'

Something flickered deep down in the blueness. 'Want me to have a word with him?'

'No thanks.' She softened the refusal with a smile. 'I told you I handled it. He won't be bothering me again.'

'Maybe.' From the sound of it he wasn't fully convinced. 'You sure you don't want that drink?'

'Quite sure.' One hand came out instinctively to smooth his cheek. 'You're so good to me, Paul!'

'It isn't difficult.' A certain gruffness infiltrated his voice. 'Sometimes I think I'm the only one who knows the real Karen Greer.'

Guilt kept her silent. All she could do was smile and go. If she told no one else the truth, eventually she was going to have to tell Paul. She owed him no less. What he would do about it she couldn't begin to guess.

The dress she wore that evening was cowl-necked and form-fitting, the silky white jersey material falling gently over her hips to the floor. Charlie clapped her hands when she saw it.

'Almost medieval,' she exclaimed. 'An excellent choice!' She sniffed delicately, brows lifting. 'Is that *Promise* you're wearing?'

'Oh, Lord!' Gail was genuinely caught out. Her eyes sought Paul's in apology. 'I had some in my hand case. I didn't think.'

'There's no one here going to steal it for analysis,' he said easily. 'Though I'd prefer you didn't carry it around with you until after the launch. My fault for not checking. Naturally we've been using it on set.' The last to his employer herself.

'And so I should hope!' She smiled reassuringly at Gail. 'As Paul says, no harm done. Just make sure you don't wear it in public. Having said that, I'm gratified to know you obviously like it enough to want to wear it.'

'I love it,' Gail assured her truthfully. She laughed, eager to make amends for the gaffe she had committed. 'It makes me feel every inch the femme fatale!'

'Coals to Newcastle,' came the dry comment from behind. 'You should maybe ask Jerry how he feels about promises.'

Gail was unable to stop the hot wave of colour running up under her skin. She could only be thankful that the four of them seemed to be temporarily isolated from the rest of the gathering. Meeting Charlene's eyes, she was surprised to read a certain empathy in the older woman's expression.

'It takes two,' came the equally dry rejoinder as her grandson moved to her side. 'Jeremy never was satisfied with what he already had.' Her eyes still held Gail's. 'It comes as no shock. Paul put me fully in the picture the day I picked you out as Cassie Bailey's successor. If you'd still been seeing my grandson it might have made a difference, but under the circumstances I saw no reason to change my opinion.'

'Thank you.' It was all Gail could find to say.

'As for you, Luke,' the other went on equably, 'it's more than time you stopped trying to smooth your brother's path. If Brenda can't hold him then there's nothing you can do about it. Being given the elbow by this young lady here might be just the medicine he needs. He seemed remarkably subdued when he came down last weekend.'

'He's better out of it, I agree.' Luke sounded unrepentant, the grey eyes hard as they rested on Gail's face. 'Congratulations. That blush was almost convincing!'

'Don't you think this has gone far enough?' put in Paul very quietly. 'Karen is vital to our profit margins.'

Luke shook his head, lip curling. 'She's not going to walk out on you no matter what.'

'Darling, I'm feeling dreadfully neglected!' Lorraine arrived at his side, sliding a proprietary arm through his, the bare whiteness of it emphasised by the blackness of his sleeve. Her smile was for him and him alone, although she did spare Charlene an edge. 'You won't mind if I drag him away?'

She was wearing a sheath of some shiny dark red material cut to a deep V which barely skimmed her nipples and finished somewhere in the region of her navel. Overstated, Gail privately thought: from the fleeting expression in Charlene's eyes, she agreed.

'Take him, by all means,' said the latter blandly. 'He's a free man.'

There was no telling what Luke's reaction might be from his face, but he allowed himself to be led off by the red-head. Gail watched them go, looking back to find Charlene watching her with a certain shrewd assessment.

'*She* won't last long,' she stated flatly. 'Not that any of them ever do. Neither of my grandsons is strong on stamina, I'm afraid. It's perhaps as well Luke hasn't married.' She seemed to catch herself up there, glancing at Paul with a faint wryness. 'No offence intended.'

He smiled. 'None taken.'

The evening progressed favourably enough from there. Gail stuck close to Paul, although the two of them moved freely among the other guests. Luke made no further attempt to come near her. With Lorraine clinging to him like a shadow there would have been little opportunity even if he had wanted to seek her out. Gail tended to agree with Charlene's assessment of that relationship. The woman was over-possessive. Nevertheless, she felt some sympathy for her. When Luke wanted out he would drop her like a hot potato.

Her own decision time came later when Paul made it clear that he would like to share her room and bed for the night.

'No strings attached,' he said outside her door. 'Just a mutual indulgence of need. We'd both enjoy it.'

'We might,' Gail told him gently, 'but it isn't going to happen. I've too much respect for you, Paul, to pretend something I don't feel.'

'Respect I can do without,' he growled, but there was a wry acceptance in his smile. 'I guess I just don't have what it takes.'

There was no point in being less than honest. 'Not for me,' she agreed. 'Can we stay friends?'

'We have to—for the next week or so at least.' He studied her, taking in the silver-streaked hair, the darkened green of her eyes, the rueful line of her mouth, resignation in his shrug. 'You and Luke,' he said unexpectedly. 'You've met before?'

'No.' Gail kept her tone steady. 'What makes you ask?'

'The way he spoke tonight.'

'That was because of his brother. And I'm not making any excuses.'

'I didn't ask for any.' He bent forward and kissed her lightly on the cheek. 'Friends, it is—for now. I don't give up hope altogether.'

Short of reiterating her former denial, there was nothing Gail could say to that. Murmuring good night, she slipped into her room and closed the door. Paul was worth two of Luke's kind any day of the week, she thought depressedly as she prepared for bed, so why was it only the latter who could stir her blood? If he had been the one asking to spend the night with her she would have had a great deal more trouble in saying no and meaning it. If he came through that door right now she doubted if she could find the strength of mind to turn him out. Not that it was likely. By now he would be all tucked up with the delectable Lorraine.

The pang that ran through her was all too obvious in its origins. Detest the man she might, but she still wanted him. Her whole body felt weak with the longing.

The weekend ran its course. Back in London again there was little time for thinking about anything but work. The end of the month would see the launch. The renewal of her contract with Rivas depended entirely on initial results. In the meantime she sat back and waited.

Payment for this job, as all the others, had been in Karen's name. Whilst willing to take the risk of copying her sister's signature in order to pay in the cheques to her bank, Gail had no intention of using the same procedure to draw any money out. Fortunately, the account Karen had opened for her at another branch was still relatively untouched, although with the quarterly rent due in a couple of weeks time it certainly wasn't going to stay that way. In all probability she would have to use some of her own savings to top up the amount required—unless Karen was back by them. There had to be a limit to how long this whole state of affairs could go on.

She had washed her hair and was sitting in a robe with a towel wrapped round her head when the doorbell rang on the Wednesday evening. It couldn't be Paul, she thought wearily, going to answer it, because she had told him she was having an early night. It couldn't be Karen either because she had her own key. Surely not another of the erstwhile boyfriends?

The last person she had been expecting to find outside was Luke. For a moment she just stood there looking at him, face totally blank.

'Do I get to come in?' he asked sardonically.

'Why?' The word was forced from her.

'Because I need some information only you can give me.'

Gail pulled herself together, slipping into the role she had practised so often these past weeks. 'In that case perhaps you'd better.'

She was slow in closing the door after he had passed her, standing for a brief moment with her hand still clasping the knob before nerving herself to turn and face him. 'You know where the living room is,' she said, and saw his eyes narrow suddenly. 'You were here the night you drugged my sister,' she tagged on swiftly before he could speak. 'Just make it quick, will you? I'm supposed to be resting.'

He ignored the injunction, moving on ahead of her into the room to stand with hands thrust into the trouser pockets of his pale grey suit as he cast a succinct glance around.

'Do you want a drink?' Gail asked. 'I think there's some whisky.'

He looked at her before answering, taking in the slight shine of her skin beneath the twisted white towel before sliding his gaze down over her body to her bare feet. Gail resisted the urge to tighten the belt of her robe and pull the material closer about her, knowing Karen wouldn't even have considered such action. The fact that she was wearing nothing under the robe must already be more than apparent. No doubt he was accustomed to seeing women in far less. He had seen her in less, if it came to that, but she wasn't to know it.

'No thanks,' he said. 'I came to get your sister's address.'

Her stare was nonplussed. 'Why?' she demanded at length, playing for time to think.

'I owe her an apology.'

'I'll tell her,' she said, not believing a word of it. 'I'm sure she'll be overwhelmed!'

'I prefer to do my own telling.' The tone was level but with an underlying determination she could not ignore. 'Don't make things difficult, Karen.'

'*Me* make things difficult?' Her laugh held incredulity. 'For sheer nerve you really beat all! What makes you think Gail would be interested in anything you had to say?'

'I didn't say she'd be interested, I just want her to hear it.' There was a hard glitter in his eyes. 'You're stalling. I wonder why? Could it be you can't give it to me because it doesn't exist?'

Her heart jerked painfully. Perhaps she had come close to convincing him the other day, but he was far from it now. She wondered where she had left a loophole.

'I wouldn't give you the time of day,' she came back on a taut note. 'Get out of here!'

His movement was swift, her reaction just a little late. She felt his hand fasten into the collar of her robe as she swung away from him, felt it dragged halfway down over her shoulders in her desperate attempt to pull free. Only the tied belt stopped it from coming open and sliding all the way off. Swung round to face him she put everything she knew into expressing her contempt.

'Trying to make the whole family, are we?'

Whatever it was he had been about to say was bitten back, his teeth coming together with an audible snap. The hand still holding her collar tightened again, hauling her closer to bring her mouth within reach. Half-suffocated, Gail felt her belt slide open and the robe give way, hanging down from her arms in imminent danger of falling all the way to the floor.

The towel about her hair had already done so, leaving a damp tangle on her bare shoulders. His other hand came up to fasten into the thickness, pulling back her head until her lips opened on an involuntary cry of protest. A wave of heat seared through her as his tongue thrust inside, stiffening her whole body with a tension that had little to do with rejection. Blindly she started kissing him back, the hands that a moment before had pressed him away now drawing him closer, her calf muscles tensing as she rose on her toes to be nearer his height. Feeling the sudden stirring of his body against her, she knew it was already too late to draw back.

He slid the robe from her before lifting her up to carry her through to the bedroom. The light she had left on the bathroom threw a shaft through the half-opened doorway to fall directly across the bed. Luke made no effort to go and close the door, laying her on top of the duvet and standing back to take off his clothing. She watched him helplessly, torn between the urgency of desire and the reality of what was happening. Luke felt nothing for her but contempt but he was still about to take her. How could she even consider allowing it when she knew what was in his mind?

'Don't you dare!' he growled when she started to move. 'You asked for it, don't think you're going to get out of it now.'

'The way Gail asked for it?' she flashed, sitting up despite him. 'What kind of man are you?'

'The kind who can give you a run for your money,' he came back tautly as the last garment dropped to the floor. 'You might have played fast and loose with Jeremy but you're not doing it with me!'

She twisted towards the far side of the bed as he moved towards her, but he was faster. Slinging her none too gently on to her back again, he threw a leg across her to hold hers still, leaning on an elbow to run a calculated glance down the length of her body. 'So much alike,' he taunted. 'So very much alike!' He put his free hand to her right breast, cupping it from beneath while the long, lean fingers slowly caressed, his eyes assessing her reactions. 'It feels the same—I wonder if it tastes the same?'

The shudder running through her was not from dread. If there had been any desire to draw back from this it was all but gone. She put both hands behind his head as he bent to gently mouth her nipple, holding him to her even as her body squirmed to escape the unbearable sensation; sliding them down over the strong broad back to trace the narrowness of his waist, trailing her fingers across the arch of his hipbone to the tensed muscles of his stomach and hearing the sudden intake of his breath.

Karen would have few inhibitions; Luke would expect none. She gave herself over to instinct, pressing her lips to one taughtly muscled shoulder then down across his chest in feather-light kisses. His skin was damp, filling her nostrils with its emotive male scent, tingling her tongue where it touched. He came on his knees above her, his hands parting her thighs, his mouth a torment she could scarcely sustain. There was so much she wanted from him; so much she wanted to give him. There just wasn't going to be enough time.

She was ready for him the moment he came into her, hips rising to meet him with an eagerness that carried them both over the crest. Gasping, still not fully sated, she felt his full crushing weight for only bare moments before he rolled on to his side, taking her with him to hold her close up against his body while his lips sought hers again.

'You don't leave a man much option,' he murmured

against the corner of her mouth. 'Give me a few minutes and we'll do that again.'

He wasn't overestimating himself; already there was proof of that. Gail pressed her face into his shoulder as his hands roved her flesh, only now beginning to consider the consequences of what she had not only allowed but actively encouraged to happen. Luke had taken her because she had taunted him, and she had taunted him because she had wanted him to do just that. Self-indulgence at the cost of self-respect, that was the outcome.

'Don't go cold on me,' he said softly when she made no move to respond to his caresses. 'We only just got started.'

'You perhaps,' she retorted, turning suddenly away from him. 'I've had enough!'

An arm pinned her back to the bed before she could start to rise. His smile had nothing soft about it. 'You've had enough when I say you've had enough, and that won't be yet for a while. I'm beginning to see what Jerry was up against—in more ways than one!'

Tell him the truth, urged a voice at the back of Gail's mind, but the words wouldn't come. He hadn't believed her before; there was even less chance now. How could she hope to explain this charade she had been playing?

He began kissing her again, this time more slowly, teasing her with lips and tongue until she had to respond in kind. His hands moved over her body, fingers tips finding all the most sensitive spots with unerring aim, making the blood throb in her ears.

When he turned on his back she was drawn along with him, her lips seeking him, cherishing him, prolonging the contact to a point where he could no longer contain the groan dragged from the depths of his being.

She felt him take her hips in a firm clasp, felt the whole hard length of him beneath her, then he was part of her again and they were moving in accord, soaring up to hover for a timeless moment at the very peak of the mountain before beginning the long fall back to earth.

Gail was still wrapped in his arms when she awoke, her cheek resting against his chest. He stirred, murmuring something under his breath when she moved, but he didn't waken. Cautiously, she slid from his grasp, rubbing the side of her neck to ease the slight stiffness. The fingers of the bedside clock stood at 12.45, which meant they had slept for more than three hours.

Hardly surprising considering the energy they must have expended, she reflected with irony. She supposed she should be filled with shamed regret, but the experience had been too memorable for that. As Karen, she could afford to ignore the dictates of convention and acknowledge her baser needs. Gail was the one who needed respect from a man.

Luke's clothing was scattered where he had dropped it. She went to pick the garments up, folding them neatly over a chair. He still lay supine, one forearm bent up and back to support his head, body relaxed. Gail stood for a long moment appraising him, feeling her pulses stir afresh as her eyes skimmed the lean and muscular body. The emotions he aroused in her were more than simply physical, she had to admit. She wanted to be with him as a person, to discover the man inside the virile male. There had been moments back at the cottage when he had come close to forgetting who she was and why she was there— moments when something with deeper connotations had flared between them. Falling in love with him would be both foolish and futile under the circumstances, yet she knew she was already half way to doing just that.

Her robe lay on the floor in the living room. She put it on, tying the belt tightly about her middle. A cup of coffee might help, although there was little chance of any further sleep while Luke remained in the flat. She wondered what she was going to say to him when he did waken—what he might say to her. In all probability he would find no difficulty. This was a scene he must have played many times before.

The coffee proved a comfort of sorts. She was sitting with the mug clasped between both hands when she heard movement from the bedroom. Luke came through a moment later, a sheet draped toga style about his body. With his hair raked through by a casual hand and his jawline showing a distinct shadow, he seemed somehow less unnerving. The grey eyes rested on her without noticeable censure.

'Any more of that going?' he asked.

'I'll get you some.' She put down her own mug on the low table and got up. 'Why don't you sit down? It won't take a minute.'

He had taken her advice when she returned. Accepting the fresh mug from her with a brief word of thanks, he waited until she had regained her seat again before saying calmly, 'You realise this isn't going to be the end of it for the two of us? We've a whole lot more to give each other.'

Face expressionless, she said, 'Are you suggesting I should become one of your women?'

'Not in concurrence,' he responded without turning a hair. 'Any more than I'd expect you to entertain other men while we're together.'

'Together? You mean you'd expect to move in?'

His glance went around the room, the twist of his lips indicative of his answer. 'Not quite what I had in mind. We both need some independence. I was using the term figuratively.'

'For how long?'

He shrugged lightly. 'As long as it lasts.'

'You mean until you decide enough.' Gail was speaking tonelessly, not really accepting the situation for real.

'If I was first to lose interest, sure. You'd have the same option.'

'Very fair-minded of you.'

He studied her for a moment before responding. 'There's no compulsion. If you don't like the idea just tell me straight.'

Like the idea? Gail wanted suddenly to laugh. If liking the idea was all she had to worry about there would be no problem. The very thought of making love with Luke on a regular basis made her heart speed its beat. Yet how could she possibly risk saying yes? Karen might return any time without warning, and where would that leave her? Not a great deal worse off than she was right now, came the ready answer. Which was true enough on the face of it. Luke wanted her on a purely physical plane, nothing else. He wasn't even bothering to pretend there might be anything else.

'What about Jeremy?' she asked, struggling to stay rational about things.

Some fleeting expression came and went in the grey eyes. 'What about him? He had his chance. He didn't stay the course.'

'It doesn't bother you that your own brother ...' Her voice trailed away before the grimness of his smile.

'Let's have a mutual agreement on that point. You don't mention him again, and I won't.'

'It still doesn't alter the facts.'

'The only fact I'm interested in right now,' he said with deliberation, 'is yes or no. Either you want to repeat what we both enjoyed through there or you don't. I'm not prepared to go into debate over it.'

Gail said softly, 'You're a louse, do you know that?'

'I've been called worse.' He waited, one eyebrow lifting sardonically at her hesitation. 'So, which?'

'All right.' She hadn't meant to say it; she simply couldn't stop herself. 'Just providing you stop seeing that red-head.'

'I already did.'

He meant it; she could tell that from the flat intonation. For a brief moment she knew a pang of sympathy for the other girl. Hardened Lorraine might be, but she had been in deep enough to feel some pain. Her own turn would come sooner or later, there was nothing surer. With Luke nothing lasted.

It made little difference right now. She too was in over her head. She would take what she could get of him and be damned to the future. Life was for living not worrying over eventualities.

'Come on back to bed,' he said softly, putting down the empty mug. 'We may as well make a night of it.'

They made several nights of it that first week alone. Waking up in the mornings to the sight and feel of this man who was fast becoming the hub of her immediate universe, Gail would lie with bated breath for several minutes devouring the strong firm lines of his features while her mind recalled the details of their love-making. A couple of times he woke first, rousing her from sleep to passion with the ease of long practice, watching her come alive in his arms with the mocking smile slowly widening his lips. She was riding a wave that had to break, but while it held firm there was no sensation to match it.

Paul was swift to recognise the changes in her.

'Who is it?' he asked the night they wrapped up the last studio session. 'Luke?'

Gail looked at him wryly, conscious of the rueful note in his voice. 'How did you guess?'

'It was obvious there was something between you last weekend, though I wasn't sure what.' The vivid eyes were all too perceptive as they moved over her face. 'You look like a woman in love,' he said softly. 'Does he return the feeling?'

She made herself smile and lift her shoulders. 'You've known him longer than I have. Is it likely?'

There was a pause before he answered. 'It happens to all of us some time or other.'

'Only you doubt if it's here and now for him.' It was a statement not a question. 'I doubt it too.'

'Because of Jerry?'

'Among other things.' The way was open for her to tell him the truth but she couldn't bring herself to do it. So long as she kept that secret to herself there was no way Luke could get to hear it. The day he discovered the deception would be the day they were through, and that was something she couldn't bear to think about.

Luke wasn't with her the morning the letter arrived. Staring at the South American stamp, Gail prayed as she had never prayed before. It was several minutes before she finally nerved herself to open it, eyes skimming the single page of scrawled script with mounting relief. Karen was fine, and having a whale of a time, but her plans had not yet, it appeared, reached fruition. They were going to Venezuela where this Drew of hers owned a ranch. Perhaps there she would be in a better position to bring pressure to bear. Another week or two might make all the difference.

Not one word of enquiry about how she was coping, yet Gail couldn't have cared less. Karen's original two weeks had already stretched to more than a month; who was to say how long it may take her to broach the subject of her future. There was no address given so she could hardly write back and tell her of the future already assured. No point anyway until after the launch. Perhaps *Promise* wouldn't sell, in which case they would both be back to square one. In this game it all depended on results.

CHAPTER SIX

It took the phone call from her father to jerk Gail into the realisation of just how desulatory she had become about keeping in touch with home. Wasn't it time she paid them a visit? he asked, sounding so tentative about it she couldn't bring herself to find excuses.

She told Luke she had to go to Scotland for a few days to see her mother who was ill, relieved yet disconsolate too that he appeared to accept the loss of her time and company without particular regret. There was a chance he was already growing bored with her, although nothing in his attitude had so far suggested as much. Their love-making got better not worse—at least it did for her. She reassured herself with the thought that when Luke wanted out he would make no bones about it.

She left on the Friday, refusing Luke's offer to drive her to the station with some quip about hating railway partings. By teatime she was greeting her father who had come to pick her up from Garfield station in the family saloon.

'I rather hoped Karen might have had a change of heart and come with you at the last minute,' he admitted ruefully when they were driving away. 'Obviously she still doesn't feel able to forgive.'

'She will eventually.' Gail assured him, hoping that was true.

He slanted her a glance. 'I gather you've made no attempt to see your mother?'

'Not yet.' With everything else that had happened these past weeks, there had been little time to even think about that aspect. It was certainly not the moment to mention that Karen herself had not been in contact with her mother for two years or more. She added gently, 'Like Karen, I have a lot of adjustments to make. How's Mom?'

'She'll be better for hearing you call her that still.'

Gail shook her head. 'She'll never be anything else. How can she be! It takes more than a name to make a parent.'

'You're right, of course.' James Branstead made an effort to sound matter-of-fact about it. 'Perhaps one day we can all get together and make our peace.'

Anne Branstead was waiting with tea ready on the table when they walked into the comfortable semi-detached that had been Gail's home for as long as she could remember. Her embrace was warm.

'I'm so glad you could make it,' she said frankly when they happened to be alone for a moment or two 'Your father has been a very worried and unhappy man since you left. Is there any chance that Karen will ever be willing to let bygones be bygones?'

'I don't know.' Gail felt bound to be honest about that much at least. 'At first I felt I should go and see my mother just because she is my natural mother, until I realised that duty doesn't come into it. She can't ever have wanted to see me.'

'You can't be sure about that,' came the level response. 'Perhaps, like your father, she felt bound to keep faith with the bargain they made. They were wrong to do it, both of them, but it's always easier to recognise mistakes in retrospect. You could call me an accessory too, because he told me the whole story before we were married and I just let it pass.' Her smile was wry. 'I don't think I'd have wanted to cope with the complications entailed in trying to get the two of you back together There was even the possibility that your mother might have finished up with custody of you both in the end.'

'It doesn't matter,' Gail assured her 'Not anymore. Everybody makes mistakes.' And if you knew some of mine, she tagged on mentally, you'd never believe it.

They were half-way through tea before Karen's name was mentioned again.

'She's doing very well, isn't she,' commented her father, sounding anything but casual about it. 'We keep seeing her name mentioned in the newspapers, and that magazine your mother takes is running a full-page advertisement for some shampoo or other.' His glance rested on Gail, not wholly in approval. 'It was a bit of a shock when I saw you at the station. The likeness is almost too much. What made you decide to alter your hair?'

'Expedience,' Gail admitted truthfully. 'Before Karen was offered this big contract with Rivas, we were contemplating a double act.'

'And now?'

She made herself shrug lightly. 'It altered things, but I still had my own line of work to fall back on.' She hesitated the briefest of moments before adding to the list of truths, half-truths and prevarications. 'I make enough to live on. Eventually, Karen plans to back me in opening my own salon.'

'In London?'

'Probably. It all depends.'

'That will be wonderful for you,' put in Gail's stepmother swiftly and warmly as her husband fell silent for a moment. 'All the luck in the world!'

James Branstead summoned a smile. 'Yes, good luck, of course.' This time the pause was briefer. 'This Luke Prentis—the writer. Do you know him too?'

Gail had stiffened involuntarily at the mention of Luke's name; she could feel her stepmother watching her with an odd expression. 'Yes,' she said at length, seeing no point in denying it. 'His name is really Richmond. He's the Rivas President's grandson.'

'Oh, I see. Important to Karen's future then?'

'I suppose so.' She met her father's eyes across the table and tried to sound casual about it. 'How did you know about him?'

'The gossip columns,' he said dryly. 'Not that I usually read the diary pages myself.'

'There was a piece about them the other day,' Anne cut in a little defensively. 'Nothing derogatory, just mentioning that they were seeing a lot of each other.'

Gail hadn't seen the item herself, but knowing which newspaper her father took, she could imagine the innuendo. She summoned a smile. 'They're two grown-up people, Dad.'

'I suppose they are.' He sighed and shook his head. 'I just don't like to think of you becoming mixed up in that way of life. If you could find your own place to live . . .'

'It isn't so easy in London,' she defended quickly 'Prices are so high.'

'If it's just money . . .'

'No.' The negative was too abrupt; she made some effort to qualify the refutal. 'Karen needs me—we need each other. Luke doesn't live in at the flat. He has his own apartment in town.' Plus a worn-down cottage in the country, she could have added. It all seemed so far removed now; as if it had happened to another person. It *had* happened to another person, came the mental rider. The Gail Branstead of those days was dead and buried.

By unspoken consent the subject was shelved for the rest of the evening, although Gail knew her father was not at all happy about matters as they stood. What she had to hope was that he would not take it into his head

to come to London to see for himself how things were.
That would be disastrous!

Sunday was one of those lovely cold bright days that
herald an early English spring. After lunch, Gail put
on slacks and a thick white sweater and went out to
walk the length of the valley which skirted the suburb.
Others had had the same idea. She was relieved to
meet no one she knew during the course of the
afternoon.

Tomorrow, or Tuesday at the latest, she was going
to have to return to London, she knew. Missing Luke
the way she did, she wanted to go back, yet dreaded it
too for the problems which still awaited her. If only
there was some way of merging one person with the
other—some way even of convincing him that she
wasn't the kind of character she had made herself out
to be. Too late, of course. He would simply wonder
what new game she was playing. She had forged her
own cage and now must dwell in it, until such time
when it was no longer possible. What she would do
when Karen did return was totally beyond her to
contemplate.

Dusk was less than half an hour away by the time she
turned into Storrs Road again. Immersed in her
thoughts, she scarcely heard the car that slowed down at
the intersection behind her to take the same turning,
only becoming aware of its creeping length at her side as
she walked when the driver lightly pressed the horn.

Seeing Luke sitting there behind the wheel of the
all-too familiar Porsche was a shock too great for her
mind to assimilate immediately. She simply stood
stockstill in the middle of the pavement staring
through the opened nearside window at him.

'Get in,' he said, reaching across to open the
passenger door. 'I've had a devil of a job finding the
place.'

Gail obeyed because there was nothing else she could do except bolt for home—and that was hardly going to improve matters. She slid nervelessly into the soft leather seat, pulling the door closed behind her. She couldn't bring herself to look at him.

'How did you find out?' she asked in a small voice.

It was a moment before he answered, the lean, long-fingered hands resting on the wheel while the engine ticked over quietly. 'I was looking for your mother's address in Scotland,' he said at length. 'Only I found yours first.' The wry note was not imagined. 'Up until that moment I was convinced you never even existed outside of Karen's imagination.'

Gail's whole body felt paralysed, her mind too numb to cope. When she did manage to respond it was in a voice she could hardly credit was her own. 'She told you often enough.'

'I know. My only excuse is that your sister's credibility is always open to doubt.' The pause was briefer this time, his tone firming. 'I owe you an apology for what happened. It was some mistake to make. Having said that, there's no way I'll accept the rape charge. You were as ready . . .' He broke off at her muffled protest, studying her averted face with a certain enlightenment. 'Another of Karen's little jokes? I should have realised. What exactly *did* you tell her about the time we spent together?'

'No more than she needed to know.' Gail was hanging on to her equilibrium by the skin of her teeth. She made herself turn her head to meet the grey eyes full on, feeling the tremor run the length of her spine. Allowing this to happen was madness itself, yet every instinct in her fought against revealing the truth. 'No more,' she heard herself adding in the same unemotional tone, 'than she's told me about the two of you. Why were you looking for the . . . my mother's address? Don't you trust her?'

'Not out of sight.' His lips slanted at the fleeting expression in her eyes. 'It shouldn't come as such a surprise. As her twin you can't possibly be blind to the way she is.'

Her jaw ached from the tension in her muscles. She said softly, 'If you feel like that about her I'm surprised you still bother with her at all.'

'She has other attributes. Sometimes she even seems . . .' He broke off again, shaking his head. 'It isn't important.' There was another pause while he looked at her, gaze dwelling on each feature with growing bemusement. 'The likeness is uncanny. Most twins have some slight physical differences, but you two could be carbon copies!'

'Only because you never saw us side by side,' Gail responded jerkily. 'It's mostly the hair that creates the illusion. I changed my previous style and tinted mine to match Karen's the day she asked me to take her place for a couple of weeks.'

'So she could do what?'

'Go away—take a rest.'

'You mean with a man?'

Her sigh came from deep down. 'All right, with a man. It was before she met you.'

'True.' He sounded relatively unmoved. 'I gather she didn't bother to fill you in on her affairs too well before she left?'

'You mean Jeremy?'

'I mean all of them. Jerry wasn't the only fish in the sea by any stretch. How is it nobody ever knew there was a twin sister before? The two of you together could have made quite a name for yourselves.'

There was no harm, Gail decided at that moment, in telling him the whole story. It fitted the facts. 'You'd better turn off the ignition,' she said. 'It might take a little time.'

It took several minutes at least. Luke was looking thoughtful and not unsympathetic by the time she had finished. 'It explains a lot,' he acknowledged. 'That sister of yours has a defence system second to none.'

'Does it make a difference?' she forced herself to ask. 'To the way you feel about her, I mean?'

His shrug left her feeling curiously split down the middle. 'The way I feel about her has nothing to do with here and now.'

What he was really saying was it had nothing to do with her either. Gail felt hysterical laughter welling inside her; she had to struggle to swamp it down. If only he knew! Deflation came swiftly. Despite the fact that she had been under few illusions regarding the depth of his involvement with 'Karen', his apparent indifference hit hard.

'I think it's time I went in,' she said huskily. 'They'll be wondering what happened to me.'

Luke looked out through the windscreen. 'Which house is it?'

'Just down there.' Her hand was on the door lever as she said it, her heart jerking in fright at the very notion of finding herself accompanied to the door. 'I can't ask you in. They know your name.'

'My reputation precedes me?' He was smiling but not with amusement. 'Don't worry, I wasn't expecting it. I've an appointment to keep back home.'

'On a Sunday?' She hadn't meant to say it, the words were out before she could stop them. His smile came dryly.

'One day's as good as another. I've salved my conscience by making this trip. At least ...' He paused, tone subtly altering. 'Look, if you ever get the yen to come back to town, let me know It wouldn't be difficult to put you in touch with the right people. With your kind of training you'd have no problem getting started.' One hand was going to the inner pocket of his jacket as he spoke, coming away again with a small leather-backed notebook and a slim gold pen. Opening the former, he wrote swiftly, tearing out the leaf and pressing it into her hand. 'That's my address and phone number. I'm ex-directory so don't lose it.' Grey eyes held hers. 'Promise?'

'All right.' She felt breathless, barely able to credit that she was getting away with this new deception Perhaps she had missed her true vocation after all. 'Thanks.'

She got out of the car before he could say anything else, unable to trust herself not to break down and confess. Luke the philanthropist was hardest of all to take. She didn't look round as the engine sprang back to life, listening to the sounds of a three point turn and speedy departure with a confusion she couldn't even begin to sort out.

It was Friday before he contacted her at the flat. Karen would probably have telephoned him to demand an explanation for his neglect long before that, but Gail couldn't find the nerve to go that far. Her heart leapt when she heard his voice. It took everything she knew to keep her own light and uncaring.

'Been away?' she asked.

'No,' he said, 'just busy. I'll be round at eight. Where would you like to eat?'

'I'll cook dinner,' she offered recklessly, and heard him laugh.

'Don't start going domestic on me. That I can do without I'll make the choice for you. Be ready.'

Short, and not at all sweet, she reflected wryly, replacing the receiver. Perhaps tonight he was planning to tell her it was over. It would certainly be the best thing that could happen. What sense was there in continuing the affair?

Seated across from him at the restaurant table some hours later, she knew that sense had little to do with the way she felt. Never, she thought, would there be another man whose very glance could stir her to such a degree. In the dark suit and fine silk shirt he was everything any woman might want.

'Is your mother recovered?' he asked when they had ordered, mentioning her weekend trip for the first time.

Gail met his gaze without a flicker. 'It wasn't serious. I doubt if I'll be going again. How was your weekend?'

'Unscheduled,' he said. 'I went to see your sister.'

What she had been expecting from him she wasn't all that sure, but the ready acknowledgment took her aback. Recovery was swift because it had to be swift: because he would expect her to have a ready response. Her brows lifted mockingly. 'And I thought you didn't believe in her!'

'She's real enough.' The taunt hadn't touched him. 'Rather less confident than when I saw her last, perhaps, but she wasn't expecting me.'

Her laugh had a cracked sound. 'That must be the understatement of the year! Poor Gail. Fancy being faced right out of the blue with the very man who . . .'

'We straightened that out too.' Luke had not raised his voice but his tone said it all. 'One of these days that warped sense of humour is going to see you hanged!'

'It's all a matter of degree.' She paused, eyes searching his, unable to stop herself from asking the question. 'So, what did you think of my little sister now you've met her on her own ground, so to speak?'

Dark brows lifted. 'Little?'

'There's an hour between us.'

'There's a whole way of life between you.'

'You're so right.' She refused to let the coolness of that statement get to her. 'You still didn't answer the question.'

His shrug was brief. 'We barely met in any true sense.'

'Long enough to form an opinion.'

'All right.' He sounded suddenly harder, mouth just a little cruel. 'I found her a very enticing proposition.'

'You mean you'd like to take her to bed again?'

'That comes into it.' He was obviously about to add something else, then abruptly changed his mind. 'Let's find another subject, shall we.'

It was a command not a request. Gail picked up her cocktail glass and took a long swallow, striving to stay in character. Karen might very well have ignored the injunction; almost certainly she would have come back with some equally caustic comment. Her mind stayed blank, all except for that small part of it examining and re-examining every word he had spoken in reference to 'Gail'. It wasn't a lot to pin any hopes to, yet there had been something in his manner that warmed her secret heart a little. The invitation he had extended on Sunday afternoon took on new vibrations, stirring a sudden temptation. If she could transfer Luke's interest from one sister to the other she would be well on the way to solving her problems. It wouldn't matter then if Karen returned, providing the latter was put in the picture.

She could start laying the groundwork right here and now, came the thought, eliciting a frisson of mingled excitement and fear. Subtlety was the keyword. One slip and the whole fragile plot could come tumbling down about her ears. Perhaps one day, if things worked out the way she would want them to, she would be able to tell him the truth and have him understand her dilemma. One day.

Her monosyllabic responses drew no particular comment from him until they were at the coffee and brandy stage. Rolling the balloon gently between his palms, he said on a level note, 'If you're feeling moody perhaps we'd better call it a night after we get through here.'

Conflicting emotions struggled for supremacy within her. A part of her wanted to agree, to set the ball rolling in the direction it needed to take, yet desire still held her in its grip. It had been more than a week since Luke had made love to her. Would one more time really make any difference to her plans? It was too soon anyway. Karen wouldn't let go of a man so easily. There had to be a gradual widening of the rift to be totally convincing.

'Tired?' she asked, assuming the familiar taunting smile.

'No, I'm not tired.' He was watching her with enigmatic eyes. 'I'm just not prepared to contend with the kind of female tactics you're contemplating, that's all.'

'Such as?' she challenged.

'Such as trying to make me coax you round. If you're peeved because I went to see Gail, that's too bad. I'm not going to pretend I've no desire to come back to the flat with you, but sleeping alone isn't that grim a prospect.'

'If that's what you'd be doing.'

His lips thinned. 'I told you when we first started this that there wouldn't be anybody else while we were together. I meant it.'

'That doesn't mean you don't have anyone in mind for my successor.'

'It doesn't mean anything but exactly what it says. Take it or leave it. It's your choice.'

Her voice was husky. 'Damn you, Luke!'

The smile mocked her. 'Not before time you got to know the other side of the coin. Drink your brandy, darling. I like my women well primed.'

He kept up the same semi-indifferent attitude all the way back to the flat. Only when they were finally in bed did he start turning back into the lover she had known on previous occasions, yet even then she sensed a certain distance in him.

Perversely, she set out to decrease it, using every art she had acquired, every instinct she possessed; measuring her degree of success by the kindling of fire in his eyes, the ragged depth of his breathing, the involuntary response of his hard masculine body to her hands and mouth and wickedly flickering tongue.

'Don't imagine you're taking over,' he said roughly at one point, turning her under him to bring his weight to bear. 'This is where you belong, and don't you forget it!'

'Every which way,' she responded, eyes glinting emerald bright as she lifted her head to kiss his irresistible mouth. 'Anything you say, Luke. Anything you want. Just tell me. Show me. *Make* me!'

Passion flared in his eyes like something alive. He took her wrists in both hands and pinned them flat to the pillows either side of her head, driving into her with a fierceness that brought a bubbling cry to her lips. He was without mercy, and she wanted none, blind to anything but the fire searing through her, the desperate need for release. Climax brought collapse for them both, utter and complete like the cessation of life itself for a single moment in time.

He was dressing when she came awake. It was still dark outside, although she could hear the sound of traffic filtering through from the High Street. The bedside lamp was switched on, showing the time to be a little after seven.

'Why the early start?' she asked, pushing a hand through her hair as she sat up. 'Don't you want any breakfast?'

'I put the percolator on,' he said briefly, fastening his shift cuffs. 'I'll eat later.' He glanced her way as he slid into his jacket, mouth taking on a faintly sardonic slant. 'Either get up and put something on, or go back to sleep. I don't have time to indulge either of us.'

Gail drew up the sheet across her breasts without looking down, too well aware of the signal her body was transmitting. Watching him walk over to the door she felt bereft. Last night was just a memory.

'There can't possibly be that much urgency about anything at this time of the morning,' she said, trying not to sound plaintive.

'I want to get started on the new book,' he responded without pausing in his stride. 'I'm way behind schedule as it is.'

Because of her? Gail wondered. She scrambled out of bed as he left the room, reaching for the white towelling robe that was the nearest covering to hand. Luke was pouring the coffee through in the kitchen when she got there. He silently filled a second cup and handed it over, not so much avoiding her eyes as simply not bothering to look at her directly.

'When do I see you again?' she asked, leaning the small of her back against the edge of the nearest working surface. She could almost hear the reply coming.

'I'm not sure. Depends how it ·goes. I'll contact you.'

'And I'm supposed to just hang around waiting for you to call, I suppose?'

He looked at her then, a long steady look. 'If you think the strain is going to be too much for you we can always put a hold on the arrangement we have.'

Gail said low toned, 'You mean you'll give me *carte blanche* to see other men if I feel like it. Is that what you want?'

It was a moment before he replied, his expression undergoing an indefinable change. 'To be honest,' he said at last, 'I'm not sure what I want right now. Under the circumstances, it's hardly fair to expect you to stay celibate while I sort myself out.'

'You think I couldn't?'

The smile was faint. 'I think you'd have difficulty. Anyway, I'd as soon not be bound by any feeling of obligation.'

She gazed at him unblinkingly, asking herself why she didn't simply accept what he appeared to be saying and be glad of it. Because there was no certainty that his reasons were anything to do with her other self, came the obvious answer. Yet just supposing they were? What if he was interested enough to telephone her home? She had told him her full name last Sunday. All he had to do was match that with the name of the road in Garfield and directory enquiries would come up with the number.

'Let's see how it goes,' she heard herself saying as if from a great distance.

If that was the reply he had been looking for it didn't appear to satisfy him too well. There was a moment when she thought he was going to reopen the subject, then he seemed to catch himself up, draining his cup in a single swallow.

Gail stayed where she was as he moved towards the door, meeting his eyes with careful aplomb when he paused to glance back at her. If he came back to kiss her goodbye she would break down and confess, she was sure of it.

'I hope the book goes well,' she said.

'Yes.' Once again there was that faint hesitation, that same sense of dissatisfaction. 'I'll be in touch,' he repeated. 'Don't take too many liberties.'

It was some time before Gail could find the will to move. When she did it was heavily, body weighed down by indecision. If Luke had been serious about getting down to writing, he would be home all day. All she had to do was make the call. He would have no idea where it was coming from.

The morning dragged by. Twice she found herself on the verge of lifting the telephone; twice she forced herself to give the matter more thought. In the end it wasn't so much a case of making a choice but of being unable to stand the strain any longer. The more she delayed the greater the chance of Luke making that call himself—at least, that was what she told herself. Her hand trembled as she dialled the number.

The sound of his voice over the line had a surprisingly calming effect. She could even find time to wonder at her own level tones. 'It's Gail Branstead,' she said. 'Did you mean it when you made that offer to help me find a job down there?'

There was no telling his reaction from his reply, though it was certainly prompt enough. 'Yes, I meant it.'

Gail took a shallow breath. 'I thought of coming down for a week, just to look around. Will you be free anytime?'

'Whenever you want to make it.' The pause lasted no longer than a couple of heartbeats. 'How about tomorrow?

'Tomorrow?'

'Too soon for you?'

'It's not that. Just . . .' Gail broke off, acknowledging the futility in putting off the moment. 'All right,' she said swiftly before she could lose heart again. 'Tomorrow it is. What time?'

'What time will your train get in?'

She said hastily, 'I'm not sure which one I'll be taking. Sometime during the morning, anyway.'

'In that case, let's make it lunch right here at my place then it doesn't matter too much.' The smile was in his voice. 'I'm no Cordon Bleu, but I turn a fair omelette.'

Gail made her tone as light. 'I'll let you know my opinion when I've tasted it. See you tomorrow then.'

She hung up before he did, standing for a moment with her hand still resting on the receiver while her nerves steadied. Luke's London home was in a mews behind Cadagon Place, that was as much as she knew. There had been no invitation for 'Karen' to visit him there. She had to pull off this switch; she simply had to! Fail, and she lost everything.

CHAPTER SEVEN

THE taxi dropped her off at the head of the mews at her own request. Number six was about half-way down on the right hand side, its door timbered and banded in iron. A wrought iron rail edged the tiny paved forecourt.

Luke opened the door himself, eyeing her slim curves in the neat blue suit with evident approval.

'Glad you made it,' he said. 'Come on in.'

The lobby was small, yet given an illusion of spaciousness by the clever use of colour. He took her jacket and hung it in a closet before inviting her up the narrow staircase to the first floor living area.

Gail fell in love immediately with the old-world air of the place, admiring the lovely individual furnishings, the rough plastered walls, the welcoming warmth of the log fire in the wide stone hearth. The latter in particular brought back memories. Looking up, she caught Luke's eyes and felt the colour come into her cheeks because it was obvious that he remembered too. It was strange how different she felt with him here in this room under her own name. She was beginning again, and this time entirely as herself.

'Drink?' he asked as she took a seat on the curved chesterfield.

'Dry sherry,' she requested, and saw him smile again.

'Dry sherry it is. I might even join you. It will mix better with the champagne than Scotch.'

Gail raised her brows. 'Isn't that a bit extravagant for an omelette?'

'Not for one of mine. You never got to sample my cooking before.'

'The way I recall it,' she said wryly, 'I wasn't given the chance. Not that I blame you. I wasn't behaving in too convivial a fashion at the time.'

'With some cause. Anyway, we can make up for it now.'

Her eyes followed him as he went to get the drinks. How, she wondered bemusedly, could casual trousers be called slacks when they moulded the male physique in such a stomach-churning manner? She knew every muscle of that superb body—could almost feel them beneath her finger tips. She ached for him to come and take her in his arms, knowing that even if he did she wouldn't dare allow him more than the barest of intimacies. Luke might have been persuaded to believe that two people could possess the same face, but for that exact likeness to extend itself from head to toe went beyond the realms of plausibility. He knew her too well. Enough time had to pass for memory to fade a little before their relationship could progress beyond a certain stage.

She was getting ahead of herself, she thought ruefully at that point. Luke had asked her here to talk about helping her find a job, that was all. He was making amends in the only way he knew how. She must resist the temptation to read too much into too little too soon.

The omelette was excellent, the champagne in a class of its own. Gail balked at a second refill, aware that she was already too relaxed for safety. A slip of the tongue was all it would take. She had to stay alert at all costs.

'This job you had in mind for me,' she said at length. 'What would it entail?'

Luke shook his head. 'I never meant to imply I had

something ready lined up, just that I had the necessary connections to get you in with a good chance. Give me a few days to talk to some people. You said you had a week, didn't you?'

'Yes.' Gail ran a finger tip round the rim of her glass, making it sing. She didn't look at him as she added casually, 'I could always go on back home again until something crops up. There isn't a lot of point in my hanging around London on my own.'

'You won't be on your own,' he said. 'Not most of the time, at any rate.' He put out a hand and took hold of hers, lifting it away from the glass. 'Stop doing that. It goes through me.' His fingers curved her palm, making no effort to release her. 'Look at me, Gail,' he commanded softly. 'I'm not talking through the top of your head.'

She lifted veiled green eyes. 'I don't want you to feel obliged to entertain me. What about your writing? You were synopsising a new novel up at the cottage.'

'It can wait.' His smile was a promise in itself. 'Maybe you'll give me inspiration. The hero is due to get himself involved with a beautiful blonde.'

'Really?' She held his gaze. 'What happens to her?'

'It remains to be seen. The synopsis is only a rough guide not a hard and fast rule. Sometimes the characters take over their own destinies.'

The tip of his middle finger was drawing lazy little circles in the centre of her palm. Gail could feel her senses stirring, her whole body tensing to the motion. Deep down at the very core of her the embers were starting to glow, curling tendrils of heat upwards and outwards. She forced herself to draw the hand away without undue haste. 'I find that hard to believe. Surely you can control the figments of your own imagination!'

'I can always try.' He pulled the bottle from its bed

of ice, tipping it over his glass. 'Seems I'll have to finish it myself if you won't join me.'

'Some imposition,' she mocked, scarcely knowing whether to be glad or sorry that he hadn't tried to persuade her further. She got to her feet, reaching for his plate. 'I'll clear away seeing you did the cooking. A fair division of labour, wouldn't you say?'

His laugh held amusement. 'Keep getting at me and you'll rue it! Stack the dishwasher and leave it. I only bother turning it on when it's full.'

The machine was almost empty at present. Gail loaded in the few dishes they had used, then closed the door and switched on the rinse and hold cycle. Fitted with solid oak units, the galley kitchen held every imaginable aid to easy living. Mentally comparing it with the one up at the cottage she wondered again how he could bring himself to spend time there.

'Wouldn't it pay you to have the cottage renovated?' she asked when she went back to join him in the other room. 'You can't possibly enjoy living like a peasant.'

'It doesn't bother me,' he said mildly. 'I already told you that. It's only the female of the species that needs the trappings.'

She gave him a swift glance. 'Was it a woman who chose this place for you?'

The reply came soft. 'No woman ever chose anything for me—up to now.' He was seated on the chesterfield, legs stretched towards the flames. Eyes holding hers, he patted the cushion at his side. 'Come on over here.'

'I don't think so thanks.' She made a show of looking at her watch. 'I should be going.'

'Scared?' he taunted. 'Of what? There's nothing can happen that hasn't happened before.'

How often he couldn't know, she thought wryly. 'I'm not scared,' she said. 'Just careful. You take the whole thing too casually, Luke. I'm not made that way.'

He lifted one dark eyebrow. 'Aren't you taking a little too much for granted?'

'I don't think so. You want to make love to me again—the same way I want it.' She kept her tone as level as she could make it. 'But I'm not going to let it happen. That's why I'm leaving right now before you wear down my resistance.'

He came to his feet as she turned away from him, coming across to take her by the shoulders and bring her back to face him. Holding her, he searched her face, expression indefinable. 'You're looking for commitment, is that it?'

'Of a kind.' She made herself stand still in his grasp. 'You left too much of an impression the last time. I can't take it again. Some people need a little security in their lives. I'm afraid I'm one of them.'

'Supposing I offered it?' he said after a moment. 'Security, I mean. Supposing I asked you to move in here with me. Would you consider it?'

The temptation to say yes was almost overwhelming. She had to grit her teeth in order to deny the need. 'It's too soon,' she got out. 'You can't possibly feel anything this quick!'

'Don't tell me what I can or can't feel.' The injunction came soft. He studied her for a moment more before dropping his head to find her mouth with his, the move so sudden she had no chance to use avoiding tactics. The kiss was a revelation to one so accustomed to the lack of real tenderness. It didn't last long, but while it did she could only return it in kind, her hands creeping up to rest against the front of his shirt. When it finished she laid her cheek against the same spot, feeling the beat of his heart through the hard cage of his ribs.

'I'm going out to visit my grandmother tomorrow,' he said, lips at her temple. 'Come with me. It isn't far.'

Not Charlie then, but the other one. That helped. She barely contained the tremor in her voice. 'I'd like to.'

'And tonight dinner.' He laid a finger across her lips as she lifted her head. 'Nothing more than that, I promise. We'll take it a step at a time, no faster than you want to go. Okay?'

Right now she could have gone the whole distance without a second thought, but he was already putting her from him. 'I'll call you a taxi. Where are you staying?'

Something else that hadn't occurred to her. She gave him a name off the top of her head, sensing his surprise even before he revealed it in his glance.

'I'm treating myself,' she added in haste. 'I always wanted to stay at the Ritz.'

'It's not a bad ambition,' he acknowledged lightly.

He came downstairs with her when the taxi arrived, supplying the driver with the destination as he put her into the back, and handing over a couple of notes.

'I'll pick you up at eight,' he said before they moved off.

Gail sat back in her seat with mind racing, trying to work out how she got away with this one. First and foremost there was the driver to deal with. She leaned forward and tapped on the glass as soon as they were clear of the mews.

'I changed my mind,' she said. 'I want to go to Kensington instead.'

'Cost more than he gave me,' came the resigned rejoinder.

'That's all right, I'll pay the difference.'

With her immediate problem taken care of, she

turned her thoughts to the coming evening, wondering if she could phone Luke from the flat and suggest they met at whichever restaurant they would be using. Yet what reason could she possibly give that would sound plausible? Shopping could perhaps keep her tied up until six or even half past, allowing for returning to base, but certainly not beyond that. The only possible alternative was to get herself all ready, then take a taxi from the flat to the Ritz early enough to be sitting in the lobby waiting for Luke when he arrived. Plenty of people met that way. The staff would think nothing of it. And later, when it came to taking leave of him? She gave a mental shrug. Better to leave that to fate. Something would occur to her.

She was living in a dream world, and she knew it, yet she still refused to give way to common sense. If there was any chance at all of coming through this period of transition then she had to take it. The way Luke had been with her this afternoon, she had no other choice. She couldn't risk losing him now.

By seven-fifteen, she was ready and waiting in a dress of dark green jersey silk which covered her arms down to the wrists yet almost skimmed the top curves of her breasts. She was on the very point of taking Karen's silver fox from the wardrobe before realisation struck. Luke was no more blind than he was stupid. Coats like this one didn't grow on trees. Karen herself had probably acquired it as a gift from some admirer. Her own black velvet jacket would have to do instead. She was hardly going to be outside long enough to feel the cold.

The taxi arrived promptly at seven twenty. At seven-forty—a little earlier than she had anticipated—she was already ensconced in the front lobby of the hotel watching the revolving doors spill their steadily-increasing load as the evening got under way. Luke arrived three minutes before the hour, heart-stopping in a dark grey suit she hadn't seen before. He spotted her right away, his mouth curving as he came over to where she sat.

'I'm not used to having a woman beat me to it,' he said. 'Are you always this prompt?'

Gail smiled back, coming to her feet. 'I try to be. Where are we going?'

'I booked a table at the Hilton so we could look at the view if we got tired of each other.'

'How wise,' she responded, adopting the same lightness of tone. Relief flooded through her. She had been afraid that he might have decided to eat right here at the Ritz, which could have made matters decidedly awkward later on. If she handled things the right way there was no reason why he should insist on seeing her back to the hotel at the end of the evening. They would, after all, be meeting again tomorrow.

'I'm looking forward to seeing your grandmother,' she remarked in the taxi. 'You said she was a real character.'

'I did?' Luke sounded surprised. 'When?'

'At the cottage.' Her smile came and went. 'Just before I tripped and fell on you.'

'I remember that.' One hand came out fleetingly to smooth the line of her cheek. 'I was a swine.'

'You thought you had reason.' He did still, if he only knew it, but she couldn't afford to dwell on that aspect. She loved this man; she wanted him to learn to love her. Not just for her body and her face but as a whole person. It could happen, given the time and opportunity. His every gesture led her to believe that.

They had a table right beside the huge plate-glass windows in the roof-top restaurant, affording a superb view out over the city. Between courses they danced to the rhythm of the resident combo, talking about everything under the sun. Gradually, as the evening wore on, the music became slower and dreamier, drawing the dancers closer together as pairs. Here and there feminine arms crept about masculine necks, pressing the softness of breasts against the hardness of chests.

Held close in the circle of Luke's arms, Gail felt vibrantly alive, her every sense tuned to the same pulsing frequency. The combination of high heels and length of leg brought hip and thigh into intimate contact with firmer muscled flesh, rousing her to a desire she made no effort to conceal. She was stirring up trouble for later but she couldn't bring herself to think that far ahead. All she wanted in the world was right here with her this very moment.

Luke put his lips to her temple, pushing aside the fall of hair to kiss the pulse beating beneath the translucent skin. 'You're begging the issue,' he murmured. 'Is that the intention?'

She pulled herself together with reluctance, aware that she owed him some degree of honesty. 'I'm sorry, I was carried away. No, that isn't the intention. Not yet, anyway.'

'Because of Karen?'

'I suppose so, yes. Partly that, at least.'

'It's understandable. You wouldn't be the girl I think you are if you were prepared to take turns with your own sister.' He kissed her again, mouth infinitely gentle. 'I wouldn't want it that way either.'

Gail could hardly hear her own voice. 'Does that mean you're prepared to give her up?'

'I was already half-way.' He hesitated before adding softly, 'I'm not going to try making out she doesn't have what it takes anymore. She always will. What she lacks is a stable background. That's what makes the real difference between the two of you.'

'Yes, I know.' She should draw him away from a potentially dangerous subject, she knew, although there was a certain irresistible fascination in hearing him speak of what was, to all intents and purposes, her alter-ego. 'At first I was anxious to see my mother, but the feeling wore off. After all, she was the one who abandoned me, not the other way round. From what I do know of her, I don't think I'd care for her very much. Blood isn't that much thicker than water when it comes right down to it.'

'I agree,' he said. 'I think you're better off leaving things the way they are. If she'd let two years pass without even bothering to contact the daughter she did bring up, I'd say she isn't worth much heartache.'

It took a moment for that to register. Gail's head jerked up. 'Are you saying Karen didn't go to Scotland this last weekend after all?'

'I'm saying it's unlikely.' The grey eyes were steady. 'Not that it matters either way now. I'll tell her first thing Monday.'

'Over the phone?'

'No, not over the phone. I don't work that way.'

'I should have known that.' Her eyes were luminous. 'Do you plan on telling her about . . . me?'

He smiled a little. 'I have to, don't I? She's going to find out sooner or later. I'd as soon have things open and above board.'

Conflicting emotions kept her silent for a moment or two. Only when she had a grip on herself again did she venture any further comment. 'Does that mean you anticipate a fairly lengthy relationship where I'm concerned?'

'Hopefully.' He sounded amused but in no way derisive. 'You're another proposition altogether, Gail. If you'll excuse the cliché, every man has his Waterloo.'

He was talking about marriage, she thought dazedly Perhaps not right away but certainly in the not too far-distant future. She had believed him not the marrying kind, and been prepared to accept it that way. Marriage was a permanent commitment—at least, it would be for her. She needed to be without a single shadow of doubt.

They had come round close to their table again. Luke took her hand and led the way from the floor, pulling out her chair and seeing her seated before taking his own seat. 'Tell me if I'm wrong,' he said after a moment, 'but I thought I detected a certain withdrawal in you just then. Are we on a different wavelength?'

There was no point in prevarication. They both knew what he was talking about. She said slowly, 'I just can't believe things happen that fast.'

'You mean you don't trust me yet?'

'It isn't that.' She paused, spreading her hands in a helpless little gesture. 'Luke, you've known so many women.'

'Which surely gives me a head start when it comes to knowing what I want?' He didn't try to touch her, his eyes and voice compelling enough. 'I was fighting my instincts from the very first moment I met you in the flesh at that party. I should have listened to them then. Even if you really had been Karen, I was wrong to take the stand I did take. She wasn't entirely to blame for Jerry's marriage breaking up. If it hadn't been her it would have been someone else.' He shook his head as she started to speak. 'No, let's leave it there for now. You're right, I'm going too fast. There's no rush. We have all the time in the world.'

Fool, she thought wryly. Why had she balked? She knew why, of course. Guilt was something she was going to have to learn to live with until the day she felt secure enough to tell him the truth—if ever there was such a time.

They left soon afterwards. Luke raised no argument when she asked him to let her go back to the Ritz alone, contenting himself with a brief but forceful kiss before seeing her into the taxi.

'I'll be along at ten-thirty,' he said. 'Don't count on being back in town too early. I usually spend the day.'

As before, Gail waited until the taxi had turned a corner before giving the driver fresh instructions, ignoring his muttered comment. At least tomorrow she would be meeting someone who would know her only as herself. There was some comfort to be gained from that. Between times, she had this charade to keep going regarding her place of abode. It promised to become a pretty wearisome task.

So why not move into a hotel for the remaining few days after Luke had been to the flat for the last time tomorrow? Not the Ritz, of course—she didn't have the available funds—but Luke would no doubt accept a change of mind without question if she told him she had over-reached herself in the first place. Once this week came to an end she would be faced with the same problems, but she'd find a way round them somehow. It was amazing what the mind was capable of concocting when put to the test.

Luke's paternal grandmother lived out at Southwark on what Gail imagined might once have been called the wrong side of the tracks. The house itself stood in the middle of a long terrace dating back to the turn of the century, the Victorian façade amazingly well preserved.

Due for demolition inside the next five years, Luke advised as they got out of the car in front of a door opening directly on to the pavement, adding with a grin that they'd have to shift his grandmother by force if she was still alive by then.

The old lady was probably very little older than Charlie, Gail reckoned when Luke introduced the two of them in the neat-as-a-pin front room, yet that was the only similarity. Lucy Richmond was physically frail, her hair white as snow above her seamed features, her hands roughened from a lifetime's work. It took the indomitable spirit glinting in her faded blue-grey eyes to lift her out of the ordinary.

'It's about time you found yourself a nice girl,' she commented, treating Gail to a candid appraisement. 'Not that she's showing much sense taking up with the likes of you, and that's a fact!'

'True,' agreed her grandson cheerfully. 'But then, it isn't her sense I'm after.'

'Shame on you,' she scolded, but her eyes were twinkling. 'Don't you let him get away with anything,' she added to Gail. 'Needs a woman who'll stand up to him, just like his father—and his granpa before him!' She turned with surprising nimbleness, pivoting on the curved wooden stick. 'Come on through to the back. I'll put the kettle on. Nothing like a nice cup of tea.'

A cup of tea, Gail soon learned, was one of the old lady's main pleasures in life.

'Never even liked the smell of that coffee,' she acknowledged contentedly, savouring the fragrant brew some minutes later. 'Do you like gardening?' she added in almost the same breath.

Gail smiled and shrugged. 'I never really did any. My father's very keen though. He spends hours at it.'

'Lot of land, has he?'

'About a third of an acre, I believe, although that probably includes the piece the house actually stands on.'

Mrs Richmond nodded towards the window. 'I've just the bit you can see out there, but it's enough for me. You'll have to come back when the spring bulbs are up. It's a real picture. Isn't that right, Luke?'

'It certainly is,' he agreed. 'I'll bring her again, Gran.' His eyes were on Gail as he said it. 'Often.'

They ate a tasty and filling lunch of home-made meat pie with potatoes and peas. Afterwards, Luke was despatched to a local Sunday flea-market with a box of tattered paperbacks for exchange.

'Always did like reading,' his grandmother confided, settling back in her fireside chair with a third cup of her beloved tea. 'It's only since Granpa went I've had time to do as much though.'

'Is Luke's father still alive?' ventured Gail, receiving a surprised glance.

'He hasn't told you anything about it yet?'

'Only that his parents were divorced when he was just a child.'

'He shouldn't have married her at all. She wasn't our kind. Didn't know what she wanted half the time, although Ralph did his best by her. Bought her a nice house, good furniture—clothes to stock a shop! Had his own garage, you see,' on a note of pride. 'That's how they met, when she broke down one day and he towed her in. Wouldn't leave him alone after that. Kept coming back pretending there was something wrong with her car.' She paused, shaking her head at some memory. 'I'm not saying she didn't think anything of him, mind, just that she didn't look any further than the end of her nose when it came to thinking about leaving all her fancy friends and her big posh home. None of her family liked it either. There was only her mother came to see them married at the registry office in the end.' There was a pause and another glance. 'You've met Luke's other grandmother?'

'I've heard a lot about her,' Gail hedged. 'Did both Luke and his brother go with his mother when the marriage broke up?'

'They had to. She had custody. Jeremy was only three. Ralph was allowed to see them Sundays, only when they sent Luke to boarding school it made things harder.' Her voice took on a sadder note. 'He went to see Margot about it one weekend. Made her come away from the house in the car with him to talk about things in private without anybody interfering. They had a crash and were both killed. The courts said the boys were better left where they were. It was only after they grew up they started visiting regular times.'

'I'm sorry.' Gail's tone was gentle.

'Yes, well, it's all a long time ago now. I was glad when Luke started writing these books of his because it got him out from under her thumb.'

There was no need to ask who 'her' was. Gail said lightly, 'I can't see Luke under anybody's thumb.'

'She's President of that company of theirs,' came the prompt retort, as if that was the only answer required. 'About time she started acting her age. You wouldn't catch me going on the way she does!'

You wouldn't catch many who could, Gail conceded mentally, recalling Charlene Rivers' vivacity. The story was a distressing one. She could only feel glad that neither boy had seen fit to ignore the fact that they had commitments to their father's family.

The sound of a car drawing up out front roused the two of them from their individual thoughts.

'He's soon back,' commented Mrs Richmond, looking at the clock on the mantlepiece. 'It's not twenty minutes.'

A door opened and footsteps crossed the other room. Gail looked round with a smile on her lips as he came in, feeling it freeze in position the same way Jeremy's was doing.

The pause seemed to go on for ever, although it was probably of no more than a few second's duration. Jeremy was the first to regain his speech, his expression a study in sheer bewilderment. 'What on earth are *you* doing here?'

She found her own voice with an effort, wondering just how many more complications were going to arise from this deception of hers. At least in this instance she could tell the truth. 'I'm Gail,' she said. 'Karen's twin sister. Luke brought me to meet your grandmother.'

It would have seemed impossible for anyone to look any more stunned than he already did, but he managed it. Only as his glance flickered towards his grandparent did he bite back the question trembling on his lips and pull himself together. 'Hallo, Gran. I wish you'd let us put that phone in then we wouldn't keep over-lapping visits this way.'

'Don't need a telephone,' she said. 'Noisy things! Anyway, I like having the two of you here together.' She paused, gaze moving inquisitively from one to the other. 'Luke didn't say anything about you being a twin.'

'I don't suppose he thought about it,' Gail responded, finding the smile easier now. 'Karen's the one Rivas is using. I'm from out of town.'

'How did you meet up with Luke?' Jeremy asked, trying to sound casual about it.

Gail stopped trying to think two leaps ahead and took a chance. 'I stood in for Karen when she had to leave town for a few days.'

'Oh?' He studied her for a moment, expression

undergoing another slow change. 'You mean you were the one . . .' He broke off abruptly, recalling his grandmother's presence, substituted on a deliberately lighter note, 'You're certainly identical. Trust Luke to see the potential!'

'I'm not actually in Karen's line of work,' she said. 'I'm a beautician. Luke is going to help me find a job.'

'He's going to marry her too,' chimed in Lucy Richmond matter-of-factly. She met Gail's startled glance with evident enjoyment. 'Think I can't read the signs? Luke never brought a girl here to meet me before. He wouldn't have done it now if you weren't the one he's chosen.'

Jeremy said blankly, 'He can't have known you longer than a few weeks.'

'I only knew your Granpa two days when I made up my mind,' said his grandmother on a reminiscent note. 'Luke always did take after me.' There was a pause and a sudden change of tone. 'Karen? Isn't that the same name as . . .'

'As the woman I was involved with,' Jeremy finished for her with weary resignation. 'Trust you to put two and two together, Gran!'

'It doesn't take so much doing. It isn't that common a name.' She was looking at Gail again, conflict in her eyes. 'You said you took your sister's place for a few days . . .'

'Not with me,' her grandson chimed in again. 'As a matter-of-fact, it seems it was Gail here who did the casting off.'

'It was easier to do it that way,' Gail responded, reacting to the challenge instinctively. 'Karen couldn't face it.'

'I didn't realise she was quite so sensitive.' His tone was brittle.

'She'd got more sense than you,' said his grandmother. She shook her head, as if the whole affair was more than her mind could reason out. 'The main thing is getting you and Brenda back together again. Have you seen her this weekend?'

'I just came from there,' Jeremy acknowledged. He paused before going on, suddenly sounding a little sheepish. 'I'm moving back in tonight. That's what I came to tell you.'

'And about time too.' The relief was obvious. 'Those boys need a father. Now you start being a good one, you hear me?'

His smile was faint but it was at least an attempt. 'I hear you, Gran. Don't worry about it. I learned my lesson. Is there any tea left in the pot?'

'I'll put the kettle on again,' Gail offered, getting to her feet. She hesitated in front of the old lady, willing her to look up. 'I'm sorry you had to find out like this. I'm sure Luke would have told you himself eventually.'

'Only after he thought I knew you well enough to make my own mind up about you,' she said. She reached out and patted Gail's hand. 'You and your sister might look the same but I'm sure Luke wouldn't be taken in. Well, I'm not either. You're a good girl, Gail.'

Gail mumbled some response and turned blindly away to the kitchen. One more word and she would burst into tears. Would the deception never end?

CHAPTER EIGHT

THEY were all three of them sitting over the fresh pot of tea when Luke returned. He stood just within the doorway surveying the scene, gaze leaping from one face to another in swift comprehension.

'That saves a whole lot of explanation on my part,' he commented at length. 'Sorry, Gran. There was a chance you might have formed the wrong impression if I'd told you first.'

'It's about time you realised which member of this family you got your good sense from,' came the prompt retort. 'It wasn't your father, and that's a fact!'

'We can all make mistakes.' Luke's eyes sought Gail's. 'Okay?'

'I was the one who had the worst shock,' pointed out his brother on an aggrieved note. 'I didn't even know there was a sister till I walked in here just now!'

'It won't do your system any harm.' Luke deposited the box he was carrying on a nearby chair. 'This little lot should last you a week or two, Gran.'

'Providing I haven't already had most of them.' She nodded towards the covered teapot. 'We saved you a cup.'

'You'll poison yourself with that stuff,' he growled, ignoring the invitation.

'If it hasn't done for me in seventy-four years I think I'll last,' came the unperturbed reply. 'Jeremy is going back home to live. Isn't that nice?'

The two brothers exchanged glances. 'Good,' said Luke crisply. 'Give Brenda my regards.'

'You could do it yourself if you came round. She's

glad to see *you* anytime.' There was just a hint of dryness in Jeremy's voice. 'Why not bring Gail with you? From what Gran's been saying, they're going to have to meet sometime. I'll prepare the way if you like.'

'It might be a good idea.' If Luke had registered the nuances he wasn't reacting to them. 'Is tomorrow night going to be too soon?'

'Why not? I don't suppose we'll be doing anything else.'

Gail searched her mind for some valid excuse to escape the arrangement but could find none. Luke was well aware that she had no other engagements this week of her supposed stay in London. Anyway, Jeremy was right. If she and Luke were to develop a relationship she was going to be meeting Brenda sooner or later. By this time tomorrow Luke would have kept his promise and she would be rid of this dual personality—although she dreaded the way it had to be done.

It was mainly at her instigation that she and Luke stayed at the house right through till nine o'clock that evening, partly because she really liked his grandmother, and partly, she was forced to admit, because it cut down the number of times he would be returning her to the Ritz by at least one.

'You've made a real hit there,' he commented in the car when they finally did take their leave. 'There aren't many who'd be prepared to sacrifice that much time to an old lady, and she knows it.'

'She's a dear,' Gail could comfort herself with the knowledge that it hadn't been all for expedience alone. 'Two grandmothers so totally different!' The realisation came almost synonymously with the words themselves, freezing her blood in her veins. Somehow she made herself laugh and tag on, 'Karen was most impressed with Charlie.'

'I'd say the feeling was mutual,' he responded, apparently having noticed nothing untoward. 'Karen got to everybody that weekend, one way or another.'

'Including you.' The words were soft.

'Including me, yes—although maybe not in quite the way she initially intended.' His lips twisted wryly. 'I told myself I was going to the flat simply to let her know I was on to her, only it all got away from me. She can tie a man in knots without even trying, that sister of yours.'

Gail said huskily, 'Perhaps she'll do that again tomorrow.'

'No chance. Not now I have the real article. Someday she'll maybe find herself a man capable of dredging up the remnants I kept catching glimpses of. The two of you started life equal. It isn't totally her own fault that she finished up the way she is.'

It was a moment before she found a way of saying what was in her mind. 'Did it ever occur to you that I may not be able to compete—on a physical basis, I mean?'

This time his smile was genuine. 'No, it didn't. Remembering the one time we did get together, I'd say we neither of us has a thing to worry about in that direction. There's a lot more to making love than being adept at sexual acrobatics.' He glanced sideways at her when she failed to reply, mouth taking on a new slant. 'We're going to be married, Gail, make no mistake about it. You'll learn to trust me.'

The same way he could so completely trust her? she thought numbly. She wished she had the courage to make a clean breast of it right here and now and take her chances on the outcome, only she knew it was beyond her. Luke was too much the male to understand her reasons for letting matters get this far. If luck continued to run on her side, he may never need to know. Unburdening oneself at the cost of another's peace of mind was often a sheer self-indulgence.

It was gone ten by the time they reached the hotel. Gail pleaded tiredness, feeling a sham when Luke expressed sympathetic concern.

'Go and get a good night's sleep,' he said. 'I'll pick you up at twelve-thirty for lunch.'

That gave him the whole morning to see 'Karen'. All she had to do once he had left the flat was take the bag she would pack ready tonight and meet him at the Ritz, ostensibly having checked out before his arrival. He would be surprised but she doubted if he would query the decision too deeply if he believed it was simply a matter of money. She would ask him to recommend a less expensive hotel and actually book in for the remainder of the week. It wouldn't be all plain-sailing from there, by any means, but it had to be easier. There was still more than a week to go before the launch. By then she would have come up with a plan to cover all contingencies. She *had* to come up with a plan.

Despite the lateness of the hour by the time she did finally get to bed, she spent a fitful night. By seven-thirty she was up and dressed, fluctuating between the hope that Luke would choose to make it an early call and dread of the actual event.

He would probably telephone first to say he was coming, she reflected over coffee, although thinking about it now it seemed more likely that he should have done that yesterday in order to be sure of catching her. But he had been with her all day yesterday, hadn't he? No, not quite all of it. What about the hour between her leaving the flat and his picking her up at the hotel? He would have known then it was likely to be his only opportunity.

She got up suddenly and went back to the living room, crossing to switch on the answering machine. There were several messages, including a plea from Paul to get in touch, but only the last really penetrated: 'I need to talk to you,' said Luke's disembodied voice without preamble. 'Eleven-thirty tomorrow.'

That was all, but it was more than enough. Gail switched off the machine and stood biting her lip. Now get round this one, she thought numbly.

There was no way, of course. No matter how short Luke made the telling, she stood no chance at all of changing her clothing and getting to Piccadilly ahead of him. If she wasn't there in the hotel lobby at the appointed time it would be a natural next step to ask the desk to ring through to her room, at which point they would deny all knowledge of her. For a wild moment she toyed with the notion of telling him another half truth in that she had only been pretending she was staying at the Ritz in order to impress him, but it was only for a moment. It would never hold water.

In the end she was left with only two alternatives. She could phone through to Luke before he left home and put back their luncheon date until one o'clock, or she could simply not be here at the flat when he arrived. The first required an adequate reason, and still left room for something to go wrong, while the second at least provided time to consider the whole situation. If Karen ostensibly went away for a few days it might give rise to some consternation, yet nothing that couldn't be handled. The answering machine had more than one purpose. It would give messages as well as receive them.

Wiping the tape clean took bare moments. With a finger ready on the button, she took a deep breath and started speaking: 'I'm taking a short holiday. I think I deserve it. I'll be back in good time for the launch so don't anybody concern themselves.'

Not brilliant, she thought after playing it back, but it would do the trick. Should Karen herself return home during the coming few days she was going to wonder what was going on, but she was shrewd enough to play it by ear until the two of them could get together. If she ever managed to get this tangle straightened out, Gail promised herself painfully, she would tread a straight and narrow path in future. This was one lesson she was not going to forget.

She left the flat before eleven, terrified that Luke might arrive early and catch her in the act. By twelve-twenty, after spending the intervening forty-five minutes drinking coffee in a nearby cafe, she was sitting in the lobby at the Ritz with her suitcase by her feet, weathering the occasional curious glances directed her way from the vicinity of the desk. It was with mixed emotions that she saw Luke coming through the revolving doors. There was no telling anything from his expression. He always looked so much in command of himself.

'Something wrong?' he asked, eyes on the suitcase. 'I thought you were booked in here for the week?'

'I was.' The rueful quality was no pretence. 'I think I had delusions of grandeur. Anyway, I decided it would be a sight more sensible to hang on to my life savings. I'm sure you can recommend another hotel?'

'No problem.' He was smiling a little. 'I don't suppose that pride of yours would let me take care of any bill you run up here?'

'You already answered your own question,' she said. 'Thanks, anyway. It can wait till after lunch, of course.'

'If you like.' He bent and lifted the suitcase, smiling again at its weight. 'The kitchen sink too?'

Gail laughed. 'It's called covering all eventualities. Where are we eating?'

'Luigi's. We're not likely to run into anyone I know.' His glance rested on her face, the look in his eyes melting her bones. 'You remember Luigi's?'

'The night you plotted my downfall,' she responded, trying to keep her tone light. 'Karen's, at any rate. Did you see her?'

'She wasn't home.' He took her arm, moving her towards the doors. 'We'll talk about it over lunch.'

There was little to tell; certainly nothing Gail hadn't already seen in her mind's eye. He had gone to the flat for eleven-thirty but the bell had remained unanswered. There was no way he could be put in the picture until he tried telephoning again. In the meantime, she could only sit tight and wait.

'She has to come back sometime,' she said, wishing she could only rely on the real Karen turning up. 'Isn't it next week you're launching this new perfume?'

'They,' he corrected. 'I don't get myself involved these days.'

You're still a shareholder, she was about to say, biting back the words in the nick of time. There had to be a limit on how much information Karen was supposed to have imparted. 'Does Jeremy work for the Company?' she asked instead.

'Yes. That's how he and Karen met.' Luke looked at her oddly. 'I'd have thought she'd have told you that.'

Gail said quickly, 'She probably did. I just forgot.'

'When did you last see her?'

There was no time to consider her reply. 'The day after you dropped me off at the flat.'

'So you went home right away?'

'There was no point in my staying.' She made herself meet the steady grey gaze, hating every moment of this. 'I thought I'd never see you again.'

'I was disgusted with myself for letting you get to me the way you did.' The smile was reminiscent. 'I should have trusted my better judgment. You still have to meet Charlie. How about coming down to the launch party with me next week?'

That was one eventuality she couldn't cover, Gail reflected. She said regretfully, 'I have to be back at work on Monday.'

'Damn. I meant to do some phoning round this morning. Not that you're going to need a job if I have anything to do with it.' He studied her, mouth curving. 'Why don't we stun everybody and just get married? It would solve a lot of problems.'

The temptation to grasp opportunity while it was being offered was almost too much for her. She had to force herself to say it. 'It wouldn't be fair.'

'To Karen?' He sounded suddenly impatient. 'You think she'd give you the same consideration if positions were reversed?'

She said miserably, 'That isn't the point.'

'I know.' He was as quickly contrite. 'It's just making things more difficult, that's all. She's doing this deliberately. Probably because she guesses what it is I want to talk to her about. I left a message on her answering machine.'

It was necessary to make some comment. 'She may not have played it back yet.'

'I'll give her the benefit of the doubt. Problem is, I'm not going to have much time left to start chasing her up today.'

'There's always tomorrow.'

Luke lifted resigned shoulders. 'All right, you win.

I'll pin her down eventually.'

Not before next week, Gail told herself with a sense of reprieve.

He left her at four, having deposited her at a small but well appointed hotel on Welbeck Street. Unpacking in the pleasant second-floor bedroom, Gail could only feel thankful that tonight there would be no journey across town before they met again, no worry in case he found it necessary to contact her for some reason. It was like having a weight removed from her shoulders, although a certain amount of caution was still called for.

They would be eating after they had called on Jeremy and his wife, Luke had said, because he wanted to see the boys. Gail contented herself with a tea-tray around five, then spent a leisurely hour preparing for the evening. The dress she chose to wear was a fine grey wool in her favourite figure-skimming style. With it she teamed her darker grey coat and accessories, adding a splash of colour in the emerald silk scarf pinned at her neckline. Her eyes were almost as bright, she noted, viewing herself in the mirror before going down to the lobby. Even her skin had a translucent glow. Being in love was a wonderful therapy.

It had its effect on Luke too, judging from the quality of his greeting when she emerged from the lift.

'I was determined to be the first this time,' he said. 'Just by way of a change. You're hardly typical of the species, you know.'

'Just because I turn up on time?' she teased.

He shrugged, shaking his head. 'Don't knock it. Most men hate the hanging around. Not that you aren't worth waiting for, of course.'

'Oh, of course!' Gail wrinkled her nose at him,

responding to the quirk of his lips. 'All of five minutes!'

Jeremy's home was in Surbiton, a large and well-designed detached standing well back from the tree-lined road. The clamour which arose from within the moment the bell-press was pushed was almost deafening.

'Brace yourself,' Luke advised, grinning at Gail's startled expression. 'Two boys and two dogs make quite a welcoming committee!'

He wasn't joking. The big square hallway seemed filled to overflowing with jumping bodies, two of them pyjama clad and shining with cleanliness, the others shaggy-haired and big as donkeys. They, at least, responded with reasonable promptitude to Luke's command to 'Stay!', falling back to sit with lolling tongues and panting breath while their erstwhile partners competed for attention.

'Nigel and Nicholas,' Luke said to Gail, detaching both larger and smaller boy from their stranglehold about his neck. 'Hey, you two, I like to breathe occasionally! Where's your mother?'

'Here,' said the small, dark-haired young woman from a doorway at the rear, raising her voice above the general racket. 'Calm down, will you!' She grimaced apologetically in Gail's direction. 'Sorry about this. I didn't hear the bell in time to head them off, and Jerry's still upstairs. Luke, will you put the dogs through in the den for me? You're about the only one they take any notice of.' Her smile held an element of strain. 'Come on through and have a drink,' she invited Gail.

The comparative quietness of the comfortable sitting room was a relief on the ears.

'I only let them stay up because they haven't seen Uncle Luke for over a week,' Brenda ruefully explained, pouring the sherry Gail asked for, along with another for herself. 'I'll let Luke get his own when he comes in,' she added, sinking into a chair with the heartfelt sigh of one who had been on her feet most of the day. 'Gosh, that feels good! You've no idea how wearing that lot out there can be.'

Gail laughed. 'I can imagine. They're fine boys. How old are they?'

'Nicholas is four and Nigel almost seven.' Brown eyes sent a challenge across the room. 'To save you the usual mental arithmetic, I was three months pregnant when I married Jerry.'

Gail returned the look without a flicker. 'You must know a lot of peculiar people to be that defensive. To be honest, it wouldn't have occurred to me to start adding up dates, even if I'd known them to start with.'

There was a small silence. Brenda was the first to break it, some of the tension drained from her features. 'You're right, that wasn't at all necessary. It's just that you look so much like your sister I thought . . .' She broke off, lifting slim shoulders. 'I meant not to mention her.'

'It has to be talked about,' Gail said softly. 'We can't just ignore it. Karen was wrong to encourage your husband. If there's anything to be said in her favour at all, it can only be that she didn't stop to consider what it might do to his home life.'

'He wasn't exactly an unwilling partner.' Brenda was looking into her glass as if she expected to find some answer to her problems there. Her laugh was brittle. 'I always thought that seven-year itch theme was a joke!'

'At least he came back.'

'Oh, yes, he came back. He didn't have anything else, you see. Not after she sent him packing.' Her head jerked up. 'Except it was you, wasn't it? He told me about it last night. So he can still hope.'

'He doesn't have a hope in hell,' Gail stated bluntly. 'Not with my sister.'

'Would you tell him that to his face?'

'I don't need to. He already knows it. He probably knew it all along.'

'Then why . . .'

'You said it yourself—an itch.'

'Not the first.'

And probably, Gail thought with irony, not the last, but she didn't say it. 'I think,' she said instead, with care, 'that this might have pulled him up short. Not that I know him very well, but from the way he was talking yesterday at his grandmother's, he regrets ever having met my sister.' It was a lie, but compared with some of the others she had told, whiter than white. 'I'm sorry he did too.'

'If it weren't for you he might still be seeing her.'

'I doubt it. He isn't Karen's type.'

'Then why did she bother with him in the first place? Because of Rivas?'

'I don't know,' Gail admitted. 'Perhaps. Or perhaps he just happened along at a time when she needed somebody different. We're twins, but there the resemblance ends. We didn't even grow up together.'

'And thereby hangs a tale,' commented Luke on a light note as he came in with the boys in tow. 'Right, you two, just sit down over there and say hallo to your new aunt.'

The two in question obeyed without a murmur, the younger one's legs sticking straight out over the sofa edge as he wriggled back against the cushions. They were very much Richmonds in looks, though with their mother's brown eyes, the latter solemn and unblinking in their appraisal of this stranger in their midst.

'Are you Uncle Luke's wife?' asked Nigel, obviously having given the matter some profound consideration. 'Or are we just supposed to call you that?'

'She's going to be,' put in Luke before Gail could answer for herself. 'And yes, you are.'

'Can I be a pageboy?'

'I be a pageboy,' echoed Nicholas happily, receiving a disdainful glance from his brother.

'You're too little!'

'We'll talk about it,' Gail said hastily as a mouth rounded in a wail of protest. Her eyes met Luke's and flicked away again, unable to sustain any singular emotion. If she married Luke at all then it was going to have to be quietly, the way he wanted it, because there was no way she could cope with a family wedding. *If* she married Luke. The possibility of that happening was becoming ever-more remote. No matter which way she played it, there had to come a time when she could no longer conceal the basic facts. Her only hope lay in keeping him in the dark until his feelings for her had developed to a point where nothing could alter them. Love was fragile in its early stages, it's growth dependent on so many factors. Were she to discover that Luke himself had been party to the same kind of deception, then how might she react? Could she trust him again?

There was no answer to that question because it hadn't and wasn't likely to happen. It took a specialist to weave this intricate a web.

She was thankful that Jeremy chose that moment to walk in. He was still buttoning the cuffs of his shirt.

'Sorry not to be around when you arrived,' he said, sounding anything but. 'I was shaving when I heard the racket. Good thing I don't use a cut-throat.' His eyes went from one to the other, sliding past his wife without lingering. 'You should have helped yourself to a drink, Luke. You're family, when all's said and done.'

'I just got here,' claimed the latter on a casual inflection. 'If you're pouring, I'll have a Scotch.'

'Me too,' chimed in Nigel cheekily, receiving a mock-stern glance from his father.

'Time you two were in bed.'

'I'm older than Nick,' came the indignant response. 'He's supposed to go half an hour before me!'

'Seeing you're both way beyond your normal times, that's hardly relevant,' said Brenda firmly, getting up to deposit her glass on the coffee table. 'Come on, say good night and scoot.'

The younger boy was already fighting to keep his eyes open. Brenda scooped him up from the sofa as Nigel slid reluctantly to his feet. 'I'm fed up!' he burst out. 'Some of the boys in school stay up till midnight!'

'Some of the boys in school might be stretching the truth,' suggested Luke, keeping a straight face. 'Anyway, it would stunt your growth.'

'I'm going to be real big,' murmured Nicholas sleepily from his mother's arms. 'I like bed.'

Jeremy pulled a wry face when the trio had left, with Nigel still muttering under his breath as he trailed in the rear. 'He's been getting away with murder while I've not been here.'

'Maybe Brenda needed the company,' returned his brother on a mild note.

'She had you.' The words were faintly edged. 'You did come round to see her, didn't you?'

'A couple of times.'

'Supplying the shoulder to cry on as usual?'

There was a pause before Luke replied, his expression revealing little of what was going on in his mind. 'If she could rely on support from you she wouldn't need it from anyone else,' he said at length. 'You're not the only one with a yen to get out and see the world before you die. She's twenty-six, and attractive enough for any man to appreciate— including your own brother. You could try telling her occasionally how good she looks. You might even get to noticing how true it is.'

The younger man shrugged. 'Coming from me it wouldn't have the same impact.'

'You're wrong.' Gail felt her colour rise as both men looked at her, but she refused to back off. 'I realise I'm sticking my nose into something that's not my concern, but you were the ones who started it in front of me. I think Luke's right, Jeremy. Brenda would love to hear you say it.'

Dark brows drew together. 'You hardly know her.'

'We're both female,' she retorted, smiling a little. 'That has to give me some advantage. Egos need boosting from time to time.'

Jeremy's glance went over her, his smile reluctant. 'Even yours?'

'Even Karen's,' she said bluntly. 'Why do you think she kept changing her men so often?'

'Kept?' The voice was Luke's, the inflection curious.

'There's no reason to suppose she isn't capable of getting her fingers burnt too,' she tagged on swiftly, giving herself no time to reflect on the slip. 'Perhaps that's why she's gone away.'

'Again?' Jeremy asked. 'How long for?'

'I'm not sure.' Gail could have bitten out her tongue. There was every chance that neither Jeremy or his wife were aware of Luke's supposed involvement with the same girl. 'She'll be back in time for the launch party though, so . . .'

'When did you speak to her?' It was Luke asking the question this time, his voice retaining that same odd quality.

Gail felt her mind go momentarily blank as realisation dawned. There was only one possible reply she could make. 'I phoned the flat around tea-time. She left a message on the answering machine.'

'You didn't mention it before.'

'I . . . didn't get round to it.' She searched the grey eyes, trying to read his thoughts. There was little reassurance to be found in the narrowed gaze. Was he starting to suspect? 'Is it important?' she made herself add.

'Not to present circumstances,' he said. His smile returned as Brenda came back into the room. 'All quiet?'

'They were both asleep the moment their heads touched the pillows,' she acknowledged, laughing. 'So much for the midnight caper!' She met her husband's unresponsive glance, the brightness fading a little. 'Supper in fifteen minutes.'

Gail waited for Luke to say they hadn't planned on staying, but he made no attempt. A little late now, she had to agree, when Brenda had obviously counted on it. Taking back the errant partner was only a first step towards reconciliation; the two of them had still to find a working basis from which to make the new start. From the atmosphere existing between them, that wasn't going to be so easy.

It was not a miserable evening nevertheless. By the time she and Luke did leave round about ten-thirty, Gail felt reasonably confident that things might eventually work out for the other couple. Sliding into the car seat while Luke held the door for her, she was aware that their own reckoning was far more immediate. She waited only until they were moving before taking the bull fairly and squarely by the horns, unable to stand any further suspense.

'You're angry because I made that call, aren't you?' she said. 'I only did it because I wanted . . .'

'Because you wanted to make sure I wasn't lying through my teeth?' The tone was level but not friendly. Luke kept his eyes on the road ahead. 'You had an idea I might be contemplating a double helping, is that it?'

'No!'

'Then why?' This time he did look at her; just a bare glance. 'Why phone her at all?'

She said slowly, 'I thought if I could catch her at home I could explain the situation myself and save her having to hear it from you. She has her pride, after all.'

'So do I.' The anger was still there in him, though slightly altered in character. 'You really thought I'd appreciate having my dirty work done for me?'

'It wasn't like that.'

'There's no other way to look at it—unless you just wanted to flaunt it in her face.'

The barb was sharp, her reaction unconsidered. 'You're such a prize?'

His silence conveyed a far greater contempt than any words. Gail put up the back of her hand to her mouth, biting down hard on the knuckle. 'I'm sorry,' she got out after a moment. 'That was childish. I love you, Luke. I don't want to . . .'

Her voice died away as he brought the car to a halt at the roadside. When he reached for her she was already half-way to meeting him, lips hungry. The kiss was almost savage in its intensity, penetrating every defence. She felt his hands at her breast, the long fingers curving to her shape. Desire coursed through her, strong and sweet and familiar—too familiar.

'We're on public view,' she protested weakly, trying to gain control of her senses. 'There are people out there!'

'At this time of night they should all be home in bed,' Luke murmured, lips at her temple. 'So should we. Come back with me, Gail. I can show you how I feel about you better than I can say it.'

Her voice was unsteady. 'And you a writer. Shame on you!'

His sigh came deep. 'I take the point. Damn that sister of yours!'

At this precise moment that was a sentiment she could well have echoed. If it weren't for Karen she wouldn't be in this mess.

On the other hand, came the small voice of reason, if it weren't for Karen she would never have met Luke at all. Could she honestly say the experience was not worth every ounce of pain?

CHAPTER NINE

HAVING determined not to return to the flat for any reason until it was absolutely necessary, Gail could have kicked herself the following morning on discovering she had forgotten to pack her hairdryer. Disliking salons the way she did, there was nothing else but to fetch the darn thing, she told herself wryly as she pulled on a cap before taking a shower. She could no way go almost a week without washing her hair.

Luke was tied up over lunchtime, which at least gave her the whole day to correct the situation. It would take her less than an hour all told. No problem really, she reflected; just a nuisance, that was all. Not that she had anything else in particular to do until the evening when Luke came for her again.

Luke. The very thought of him made her ache with longing. Was it really so likely that he might stop to consider the similarities so closely when his mind had already accepted the fact that she and her twin were impossible to tell apart? She knew she was grasping at straws. Luke would know. If his eyes didn't tell him the truth his other senses wouldn't leave him long in doubt. They had been too close, too gloriously uninhibited, too recently parted for any pretence to stand the test.

It was going to be difficult finding reasons why not once he had spoken to 'Karen', she realised. Waiting for one's wedding night hardly held water when the deed, so to speak, had already been done. She shut off at that point, refusing to countenance the all-too obvious. Confession was a last resort. Something would occur.

She let herself into the flat at ten-fifteen, the faint hope swiftly dying. Karen wasn't going to be home in time for the launch; she had better learn to accept it. Even if she allowed Luke to shed his self-imposed obligations, she was still going to have to assume the role at least one more time in order to fulfil the present commitment with Rivas. After that the only solution was to have her other self vanish again, until such time when the real one decided to turn up—if ever. Gail had to acknowledge the fact that ingenuity could only be made to stretch so far. Her mind felt as if it were going around in circles already.

It seemed a waste while she was here not to use the facilities to hand. Afterwards, she thought, she might pop along to Harrods and do a little browsing before lunch. It would all help pass the day.

She was wrapped in Karen's terry robe listening to Radio One while she brushed out her newly dried hair when the doorbell pealed, freezing her hand in mid-stroke. That couldn't be Luke, she thought in panic. Not when the same message was still on the machine.

Unless he didn't believe it, of course. Unless he thought Karen was simply lying low in order to avoid the confrontation. It wasn't beyond the realms of possibility, she supposed. It might even explain why he had claimed to be otherwise engaged today after intimating he would be free all week.

Her first inclination was to ignore the repeated summons. Only when she realised that the sound of the radio might well have carried through to anyone standing close to the outer door did she resign herself to the inevitable. It had to happen sometime, why not get it over?

It was strange, but she could feel herself slipping

into a different frame of mind as she approached the door. She could even feel regret that Luke would never make love to her here in the flat again. It was going to be a long time before 'Gail' would be able to let herself go in quite the same fashion.

She had a suitable quip ready on her lips when she opened the door. Seeing Brenda standing there shocked her into momentary silence.

'Sorry,' she got out. 'I was expecting someone else.'

'Not my husband, I hope?' said the other. Riveted to Gail's face, her eyes registered a certain doubt. 'You *are* Karen?'

'The same.' Gail found the kind of smile her sister might have used. 'It would depend who your husband is.'

'I'm Brenda Richmond.'

'Ah!' The smile felt stiff. 'Then you're a little late. I haven't seen Jeremy in weeks.'

'Not by your own choice though.' Brenda was not about to leave it at that. 'You see, I happen to know it was your sister who told him to go that night. He only found out himself at the weekend when he met her again.'

'And now you're afraid he might come back to see how I personally feel about it, is that it?'

'Yes.' There was a pause before the request came. 'Look, do you mind if I come in for a moment? I feel awful discussing this on the corridor.'

Short of closing the door in her face—which surely not even Karen would have done—Gail could see no way out. She shrugged and stepped back. 'If you must. Sorry I'm not dressed. I just washed my hair.'

Brenda took a swift glance around the living room as she accepted Gail's invitation to a seat, all too obviously visualising Jeremy here. 'You could probably have just about any man you wanted,' she said on a bitter note. 'Why can't you leave other women's husbands alone?'

'I don't do the chasing,' Gail returned evenly, wondering if that were strictly true where Karen was concerned. She paused, anxious to get this over yet conscious of the other girl's distress. 'What exactly did you want to say?'

Brenda flushed, but she didn't look away. 'I want you to promise me you'll not encourage Jeremy if he does come back to see you again.'

'You don't have to worry about that. I don't have any interest.' It was out of character, but she couldn't resist adding, 'He wouldn't have any need of other women if you stopped mooning over his brother.'

The flush deepened. 'There's never been anything between Luke and me!'

'Not for want of wishing on your part, I'll bet.' Watching the other's expression, Gail knew her hunch last night had been at least half right. She thrust home the advantage, hoping she was doing the right thing. 'He's jealous—and why not? From what he told me, it's always Luke you turn to when something goes wrong, only Luke your face lights up for. What man's going to play second fiddle to his own brother?'

'It isn't like that.' The tone was low and pain-filled. 'It really isn't! Perhaps a little at first because Luke was older and more mature, and the only one who seemed concerned about what I wanted rather than what was best for . . .' She caught herself up, biting her lip. 'You know Luke too?'

'We met down at Bannerdale,' Gail acknowledged, already regretting having gone so far. 'Look, I shouldn't be saying this. It isn't my business. It's just that . . .' she paused wryly, then decided she may as well finish it now '. . . he needs to feel *he's* the man of the house not his brother.'

Brenda was looking at her oddly. 'You know,' she said after a moment or two, 'you're not at all what I expected. Why are you telling me all this?'

'I used to be a girl guide.' Gail quipped, donning the mask again. 'Why not? I've never been dog-in-the-manger about my men.'

'Not even Luke?' The question came soft—perhaps just faintly edged. 'I suppose you already know he's planning on marrying your sister?'

'I do now.' The strain was telling on them both; Gail desperately needed to be alone. 'Good luck to them.'

Brenda had risen. 'I'd better be going. I left my younger son with my mother and she's expecting me back for lunch. I'll see myself out.'

At the door she paused, glancing back to where Gail still perched on the arm of a chair. 'I think you're not nearly as hard as you try to make out,' she remarked suddenly. 'Thanks, anyway. I'll remember what you said.'

Gail let out her breath on a long sigh when the outer door closed, sliding down into the well of the chair with a feeling of utter exhaustion. It was all becoming too much for her. Far, far too much! Before too long there was going to come a point where she could take no more.

She almost reached that point several times during the rest of that week. Luke was attentive, thoughtful, generous—and increasingly frustrated by her refusal to allow their lovemaking to go beyond a certain line.

'So you're not going to sleep with me again until I've straightened things out with Karen,' he exploded on the Friday evening when she slid out of his arms with a murmured excuse that it was getting late. 'Okay, I can go along with that even if I don't exactly appreciate it, but surely to God I can at least touch you!'

They had come back to the mew's apartment after dinner—which had been a mistake, Gail acknowledged ruefully now. 'There's touching and touching,' she said, trying for a lighter note. 'You want to get me so I can't say no.'

'Damned right!' he growled. He reached up suddenly from the rug in front of the blazing fire, pulling her down to him again. 'You're driving me crazy, woman! I want to see this gorgeous body of yours, explore every inch of it, feel the warmth of you under me.' His voice softened, turning her bones to jelly. 'I want to kiss my way down the whole lovely length of you—to make you cry out and come back for more. I want to feel you holding me, urging me, claiming me, the way . . .'

'I'm Gail,' she said thickly, 'not Karen! I told you before I can't compete.'

'You could blind her,' he said. 'I can sense it in you. All it takes is the will.' He slid his hands down to her hips, fitting her to him with a singleness of purpose impossible to deny. 'That's what you're doing to me. That's what you did to me the first time I ever kissed you.'

'And Karen didn't?'

The lean features tensed beneath her eyes, then forcibly relaxed again. 'Not the same way. It would take another man to understand the difference. Are you going to keep throwing her in my face?'

'No.' Gail scarcely understood her own motives. She was talking about herself—*herself*! Karen was four thousand miles away. She lowered her head and kissed the firm lips, seeking the courage she so desperately needed. Only where did she start? What did she say? She imagined the change that would come over his face, the hardening of his eyes, of his mouth, the lash of his tongue. He wouldn't understand her motives. How could he understand? 'I'm sorry,' she said miserably. 'I can't explain the way I feel. I want you too, Luke, only . . .'

'Only it isn't going to happen.' There was resignation in his voice. His mouth stretched to a brief smile. 'My fault. I got carried away.'

She moved away from him as his hands relaxed their grasp, sitting up to push shaky fingers through her tousled hair. 'I'd better go. I'm taking an early train in the morning.'

'You could stay over till Sunday,' he said, coming upright himself. Grey eyes skimmed her face, lingering on the curve of her mouth. He groaned suddenly and put out a gentle hand to caress the line of her cheek. 'I'm sunk,' he admitted. 'Hook and line. I need you, Gail. I've needed you for a long time.'

He would remember this moment of surrender, she thought numbly: remember, and hate her for it. It was then that she finally began to acknowledge she could never marry him. Even if by some miracle she got away with this deception of hers, she would be living with the knowledge for the whole of their lives together. The best thing she could do for both of them was to break things off now before they got any worse.

Only she couldn't do that either, because she didn't have the guts. Not face to face. She had to play it through to the end, let him finish with 'Karen' the way he had planned, even attend the launch party, but once that was over both she and her supposed sister were going to disappear for a while. He would try to trace her there was no doubt, so it was all going to come out. Only she wouldn't be around to know about it. Coward, she thought contemptuously.

Her failure to respond brought a change in him,

wiping all expression from his face. His hand dropped away from her.

'I'll take you back,' he said abruptly. 'My need is obviously greater than yours.'

He didn't speak at all on the way. Only when he drew up in front of her hotel did he say with control, 'Do you want me to come to the station with you?'

Gail shook her head, not even considering the words. 'I hate station goodbyes.'

His laugh sounded brittle. 'That's something else you share with Karen—except that in her case it was probably because she wasn't going where she was supposed to be going.' He turned his head to look at her, eyes narrowed to her face. 'What is it?' he asked as if the words were dragged from him. 'What went wrong so suddenly?'

She said huskily, 'I think you want too much, Luke. More that I can ever provide.'

'You underestimate yourself,' he said. 'Me too, if you really believe I'm only interested in physical satisfaction. All right, so maybe that's the impression I gave you tonight.' His lips twisted a little. 'I never had to fight for it before. All the same, it's only a part of what I feel.' He paused, wryly shaking his head. 'I'm not too good at this sort of thing—maybe because I haven't had much practice. When I told you I needed you back there, that, to me, said it all.'

'It's been too quick. It can't last.' Gail could hear the tremor in her voice. 'Luke, I . . .'

'It *will* last!' He reached out and drew her towards him, cupping her face between his two hands with a tenderness that made her want to weep. 'Gail, I love you. I'm going to convince you of that if I have to spend a lifetime doing it. And if I have to wait to show you how wrong you are about yourself, I'll do that too. You're worth waiting for.'

Oh God, she thought desperately as his mouth found hers, it's impossible! And it was, because she was kissing him back, blind to everything but her love for this man—her need to let him know it.

He was smiling again when he finally put her from him. 'That's a good enough start,' he said. 'I'll deal with the rest when the time's right. I'm coming north to meet your family next weekend. By that time I'll have everything sorted out. I shan't ring you between then and now because I'd say a week thinking things over is just what you need.'

A week in which to compose the letter he must receive no later than Friday morning if her family were to be kept out of it, she thought numbly. Her father would be devastated if he ever discovered what she had done. Tonight was the last time she would see Luke as herself. It had to be.

She clung to him for a moment of sheer wrenching despair at the hotel doorway. 'I love you,' she said. 'I really do love you, Luke. Always remember that.'

She was gone before he could reply, slipping from his arms to push blindly through the doors.

Going home for the weekend as she had originally planned was out now, she acknowledged in the lift. Her stepmother was too astute not to realise that something was radically wrong. She needed time to get herself together first. Providing Luke made no attempt to contact her family after he received her letter—and there was every reason to believe it would be the last thing he would want to do—they need never know what a mess she had made of her life. Perhaps she could get a job as a demonstrator moving around the country. Positions like that were often relatively difficult to fill because of their nomadic requirements. Tomorrow wouldn't be too early to start looking. She had nothing else to do.

It only occurred to her later, during the long and restless night, that her face was probably already too well known—albeit as Karen Greer—to escape recognition. Even the receptionist right here at the hotel had given her an odd look when she had signed herself in as G. Branstead, although the woman had been discreet enough to make no comment, perhaps assuming that she wished to stay incognito. Should the Press latch on to the fact that there were actually two of them, which could conceivably happen, then they for sure weren't going to leave it alone until they had ferreted out the whole story. If there was any chance at all, no matter how remote, of Luke discovering the truth that way then she couldn't afford to take it. Though the letter she planned to write might underline her lack of courage, it was at least personal.

She was back in the flat before lunch on the Saturday, but it was late afternoon before she could gather sufficient resilience to start answering the more immediately essential of the phone messages. Norah was out, which offered some respite. Paul answered almost at once.

'I've been hanging around for a week!' he exploded the moment he heard her voice. 'What was the big idea walking out like that?'

Gail deliberately flattened her tone. 'I'd rather not go into it, if you don't mind. I'm back now, as I said I'd be. What more do you need?'

'A hell of a lot!' He was angry to a degree she had never personally experienced in him before. 'You've been right here in town, Karen. You and Luke. You were seen all over the place. I even know about the hotel in Welbeck Street where you were booked under another name, for what good that was supposed to do. Luke's idea, was it, or yours?'

'It wasn't me he was with, it was Gail,' she said, stepping into the familiar trap. 'My twin sister, in case you need it spelling out for you. She's the one Luke is interested in, not me.'

'Twin sister?' Paul sounded dumbfounded. 'Is this some kind of joke?'

'Not from my point of view.' She swallowed thickly, aware that the whole affair had got so far out of hand she couldn't even begin to control it any more. When Luke discovered the truth they would all no doubt become privy to the same knowledge, but for the present she had no choice other than to continue the charade. She forced a harsh little laugh. 'I got ousted by my own sister, darling. Isn't that a howl?'

The stunned quality was still right there in his voice when he spoke again. 'I'd no idea you even had a sister, much less a twin.'

'I didn't know myself until a few weeks ago. Apparently we were parted when we were babes-in-arms.' Gail laughed again, hearing the rasp. 'Better if it had stayed that way. What you don't know can't harm you.'

'What you need,' Paul said softly after a moment, 'is someone to talk to.'

'I thought that's what we were doing.'

'Not the way I mean.'

Her response was swift and instinctive. 'If you're thinking of offering your services as an anodyne, I'd rather you didn't bother thanks. Despite any evidence I might appear to have given to the contrary, one man is not the same as another!'

'If you learned that much it's something,' came the dry comment. 'It could just be I'm not on the market myself anymore.'

It was doubtful if Karen would have apologised;

Gail fought back the urge. 'Fine by me. Let me know what's on the agenda for next week.'

'I'm not leaving you to stew on your own over a Saturday night,' Paul stated firmly. 'I'll pick you up at eight. No strings. Call it good PR, that's all.'

He rang off before she could form a refusal, leaving her to contemplate the next step with a surprising lack of emotionalism. Friend or foe, Paul was first and foremost a promotions man. If she told him the whole story now he wouldn't hesitate to use it, should he see fit. So no confessions, good for the soul or not. No matter what the cost she had to see it through.

She was ready and waiting when he arrived, her dress of flame red crêpe deliberately chosen from Karen's wardrobe for its very flamboyance.

'Glad to see you can still fly the flag,' he remarked. 'Nobody's worth going into a decline over.' He studied her with a curious little smile. 'I can hardly believe there are actually two of you. My informants were completely taken in.'

'Were they on the spot by accident or design?' Gail asked.

He shrugged. 'It hardly needed any design on my part. Your face is already well-known enough to make recognition inevitable sooner or later. You were seen after you left that message, so I made some enquiries.'

'My sister was seen.'

'All right then, your sister.' He shook his head bemusedly. 'It's going to take some getting used to. Where is she now?'

'Home.'

'Which is where?'

'She wouldn't want you to know that. She's . . . a very private person.'

'Who happens to have stolen your man.'

Gail turned away, ostensibly to get her coat. 'It wasn't like that. Luke simply prefers her to me.'

'You mean he's serious about her?'

'Why don't you ask him?'

'And get my head bitten off?' Paul laughed. 'I expect we'll find out in due course.' Helping her on with the coat, he added, 'If it's your future you're worried about, don't be. Identical twins might have supplied a certain extra zest to the campaign, but it's far too late to start rethinking the whole lay-out.'

There was such a thing as last-minute surprises, Gail reflected with irony, not wholly deceived. Even if she could trust Paul, where would she start the telling? Why bother anyway? He wasn't the one whose understanding she needed.

It was a far from successful evening. Returned to the flat by eleven-thirty, Gail was more than relieved when Paul made no effort to prolong their parting. From a purely personal point of view their association was at an end. Better that way considering the circumstances. Perhaps when Karen herself finally put in an appearance the two of them might get together.

Luke turned up without prior notice on the Sunday morning. Opening the door to him, Gail felt her heart turn over. It took every ounce of willpower she had to keep her emotions locked away.

'You might have 'phoned,' she said.

'I did,' he responded tautly. 'Several times. Were you ever away, or was that just a ruse?'

Gail lifted her shoulders in calculated indifference. 'Does it matter? You're here now. Come on in.'

He followed her through to the living room, tall and lean and vital at her back. She slid her hands into the pockets of her housecoat so that he shouldn't see her nails digging into her palms, turning an expressionless face.

'There's some coffee left in the percolator.'

'No thanks.' The tone was harsh. 'What I have to say won't take long. Since when did you become a marriage guidance counsellor?'

It was a moment or two before she could think what he was talking about. 'Brenda told you she'd been here?' she said at last.

'Obviously. She also told me just what you'd said.' He drew in a breath, the anger spilling from him. 'How the devil would you know anything about what makes or breaks a marriage?'

'Putting two and two together was never that difficult,' she returned smartly. 'Most men need a reason for going after another woman. If your sister-in-law had given one thought to Jerry's feelings before running to you with her problems there mightn't have been quite so many.'

The grey eyes were narrowed. 'Has he been back?'

'No, he hasn't. I doubt if he's stupid enough to still believe there was ever any future in it where we were concerned.' Her head was up, her gaze steady, the ragged beating of her heart loud only in her own ears. 'Luke, it's over. I don't want him. I never really did want him. If Brenda plays her cards right she won't have any more trouble with him. After all, she's attractive enough in her own right—but you already know that, of course.'

He said softly, 'You're suggesting I had designs on her myself?'

'Oh, I doubt it. If you had you'd have done something about it. No, I think the two of you simply underestimated Jerry, that's all. You probably still do.'

The silence was lengthy, the change of expression slow. When he did speak again it was with rueful acknowledgment. 'It seems to be a habit of mine. Brenda said you weren't what she expected.'

'I was feeling philanthropic that morning.'

'Now that's the kind of remark *I'd* expect from you.' He was studying her with a dangerous intensity, eyes penetrating her defences. 'What is it with you, Karen? Why all the barriers?'

'Because I don't intend getting hurt,' she said flatly. 'Why not just say what you really came to say, Luke? It isn't as if I didn't have ample warning.'

He shook his head. 'It isn't quite as simple as that.'

'So let me say it for you. You're giving me up because you prefer my sister? Is that about the gist of it?'

His mouth twisted suddenly. 'You knew I'd been seeing her.'

'Of course I knew. It was obvious the way your mind was working the last time you were here.'

'It didn't seem to make a great deal of difference to the way you were that night.'

'No.' She was maintaining her grip with difficulty. Her smile came thin. 'Put that down to your inimitable technique. I daresay I'd find you just as impossible to resist even now.'

He said wryly, 'I asked for that. I'd even confess to still wanting you, Karen. We shared some memorable experiences.'

Gail smiled again. 'You don't have to bolster-up my ego. I'll survive.' She should get him out of here right now, she knew, yet some part of her couldn't let go. 'How about that coffee now? At least we can part friends.'

The hesitation was brief. 'That sounds a good idea. We still have to get through Wednesday evening.'

The launch party. She had almost managed to forget about that. 'I'll get the coffee,' she said.

In the kitchen, she leaned her head against one of the overhead cupboards for a moment, gathering her strength. Barring Wednesday, which didn't count, this would probably be the very last time she saw Luke. She had to resist the desperate need to draw the moments out. Just let him drink his coffee and then show him the door, the sooner he was gone the sooner she could start getting over him.

Get over him? That was a laugh in itself. She would never get over him. Not in a lifetime. He was part of her the way no other man could ever be.

He was sitting down when she went back with the tray, one leg crossed comfortably over the other in a pose she knew so well. He watched her pour, following the movement of her hands with an attention she found increasingly disturbing. When she handed him his cup there were two faint lines drawn between his brows.

'It's unbelievable,' he said slowly, 'how alike the two of you are. Even down to the way you lift a coffee pot with your left hand instead of the right like most other people. I could almost swear . . .'

The lobby door had not been closed. As if from a great distance, Gail heard the sound of a key in the outer lock, the cheerful hail as the door was pushed open. 'Hi there, I'm back at last!'

She was still sitting looking at Luke when her sister walked into the room.

CHAPTER TEN

KAREN was first to break the silence, her smile knowing. 'Chose the wrong moment did I? Sorry about that. There wasn't time to let you know.'

Gail found her voice, registering its tinny sound. 'The telephone was invented quite some time ago.'

'True, but why bother? I don't plan on staying long enough to put anyone out.' She dropped the suitcase she was carrying just inside the door, quirking an eyebrow in Luke's direction. 'You seem surprised—or would stunned be more like it? Didn't this sister of mine let you in on the secret?'

He dragged his gaze from tanned features back to pale ones, the realisation even now only just beginning to take shape. Gail winced at the dawning contempt, stifling the urge to start trying to explain. It was too late. It had been too late from the day she had first begun all this.

'Congratulations,' he said. 'You really had me fooled.' He reached out and set the untouched cup of coffee down on the table, turning his attention to Karen again. 'I take it you just got back from the original trip?'

'Original?' She looked puzzled for a moment, then shrugged. 'Well, I suppose so. Gail stepped in to cover for me last month. Not that I intended being away quite so long, I have to admit.' Her smile held a certain satisfaction. 'Let's just say I finished up with more than I bargained for.'

'Didn't we all.' Luke's tone was sardonic. 'Wherever you were, you obviously didn't hear about Carrie Bailey breaking a leg.'

Green eyes widened a fraction as the mind behind them leapt to an immediate and shrewd conclusion. 'And I was offered the job?' Her laugh held a note of irony. 'Well, what do you know! Lucky for me I made the right choice.'

'Lucky?' Gail queried. 'How can you say that?'

'Because I'm going to be Mrs Van Hewson, that's why! Drew asked me to marry him.'

'Superb timing.' Luke's mouth had a hard slant. 'Unlike your sister, you seem to have left little to chance. That is Van Hewson the industrialist?'

'The same.' Karen gave him a challenging look. 'I'm not sure where you fit into the picture, but if there's any reason why you'd feel like filling Drew in on my lurid past, you can think again. He already knows all there is to know. He's no plaster saint himself, if it comes to that.'

'He's been married before—twice, to my knowledge.'

'So? Third time lucky, isn't that what they say?' She was shrugging out of the supple leather jacket as she spoke, smoothing the matching pants over shapely hips in a gesture instinctively calculated to draw attention to that same area. 'Ex-wives are no problem.' Her gaze shifted from Luke to her sister, taking on a different light of interest in the process. 'I gather you got the job in my stead? Hope you made a success of it.'

'The campaign isn't due to be launched until Wednesday.' Gail hadn't even glanced in Luke's direction during the last few minutes, unable to bear the disgust she knew was in his eyes. 'What you said just now about not being here for long . . .'

'That's right. I only came back at all to clear up my affairs, as they say.' Her smile came and went. 'Some of them, anyway. Drew expects me back within the week. I'd hate to disappoint him.'

'If you're thinking what I think you are,' put in Luke hardily, 'then forget it. Whether she stays or not doesn't make any difference. You're the star of the show.'

'I never wanted to be,' Gail denied, still keeping her eyes averted. 'Not this way. I don't expect you to believe me but . . .'

'Don't waste your time.' He was getting to his feet as he spoke, the movement abrupt. 'Just be there Wednesday. Paul will bring you down to the house.'

Karen moved aside to let him pass, shrugging philosophically when he failed to make any farewells.

'Not exactly the affable type, is he?' she commented lightly as the outer door closed. 'Not that he mightn't have cause to be sore if my senses don't deceive me. Never make a fool of a man, darling—at least, not if he's likely to find out. They just can't take it. Who is he, anyway?'

'Jeremy Richmond's brother,' Gail said tonelessly, eliciting a long slow whistle of surprise.

'Really? So all that work I put in on Jerry paid dividends after all!'

'Not the way you mean. I gave him the push in your name that very first week.'

'Oh?' Karen's look was speculative. 'Then how did you meet lover-boy himself?'

'You wouldn't be interested.' Gail took up the cup Luke had left and put it on to the tray, noting with an odd detachment that her hand was steady as a rock. 'At least I don't have to worry about this place anymore. I'll move out to a hotel for the rest of the week.'

'You don't have to do that.' Karen sounded faintly nonplussed. 'You've changed, you know.'

Gail lifted the tray and made for the kitchen. 'I've had plenty of time to do it in.'

The crockery was in the bowl before Karen appeared in the doorway behind her. 'Look,' she said, 'I realise I dropped you in it turning up out of the blue like this, but you can hardly blame me for any mess you got yourself into. You should have told him the truth, not carried on pretending to be me.'

'Yes, I know,' If Karen knew the extent of that pretence, reflected Gail with irony, she would probably laugh herself silly. She conjured a smile and a shrug. 'Forget it. I'll finish off the act on Wednesday then I'm heading for home.'

'For a rest, you mean?'

'For good.'

Karen was silent for a long moment studying her sister's expressionless face. 'You don't really think anything *he* might say will make any difference if things go well?'

'It doesn't really matter.'

The sigh came long and resigned. 'It's your future.'

Gail looked round at her. 'It could still be yours.'

'Except that I don't want it anymore. I'm getting married, remember?'

'To a man you don't have any feeling for.'

'Not true.' Karen sounded more amused than annoyed. 'Drew has a lot going for him—and I'm not just talking about money.'

'He has to be a lot older than you are.'

'Twenty-five years, maybe even a little more.' There was derision in her smile. 'You haven't been running around with any naïve youth yourself from what I saw—or are you going to make out he didn't stay the night?'

'There's only ten years between us,' Gail retorted, drawn despite herself. 'Eleven at the most. In any case, he . . .' She broke off there, teeth clenching. 'It isn't important,' she got out, turning back to her washing-up. 'I'll get dressed as soon as I finish these, and pack my things.'

'Suit yourself, but I think you're being ridiculous. We've shared a bed before.'

The same one she had shared with Luke. Gail knew she couldn't. She said with control, 'We don't have anything in common so let's stop pretending. You'll get through quicker on your own.'

'You might have a point there. All the same, I'd prefer we parted on good terms. I might even get round to paying our mutual parent a visit next time we're in England. You can hardly deny I have the right.'

It might be best for him if he remained in ignorance, came the fleeting thought, swiftly shelved. Who was she to decide for him? 'Just never tell him it wasn't you who did the Rivas job, that's all,' she appealed.

'If that's the way you want it.' Karen had obviously given up trying to sort out the whys and wherefores. 'I'll make some more coffee,' she added, moving forward to reach for the percolator. 'We can at least have lunch together before you go.'

It took Gail no more than fifteen minutes to pack. Wearing the same blue jersey dress in which she had arrived that very first day, she took her suitcase through to the living room where Karen was waiting with the pull-out dining table ready set for two.

'Cottage cheese salad okay?' asked the latter, pouring coffee for them both. 'There wasn't much else in the fridge.'

'I was due to do some shopping tomorrow.' Gail placed a slim file of papers beside her sister's plate. 'Those are your bank receipts and statements. All cheques have been cleared.'

Karen took a look at the balance and whistled softly.

'Nice!' There was a pause before she said with some reluctance, 'I suppose the majority of this is really yours by rights.'

Gail shook her head emphatically. 'It belongs to Karen Greer. I still have enough left in that account you opened for me to see me through now I don't have a quarter's rent to find. I'll take that as full payment.'

'If you're sure.' Karen made no attempt to conceal her gratification. 'I'll buy Drew a wedding present with it. Something special. I'm hardly going to need it myself.'

Gail looked across at the face that was a mirror image of her own, wondering how the minds within could be so antithetical. 'You don't feel you should hang on to it as a fallback, just in case?' she asked, already knowing the answer.

Green eyes met green eyes with bland assurance. 'There isn't going to be a number four, you can bet your life on that. I don't only have youth and looks to hold him with, I can keep his mind exercised too. We're a fortunate pair, Gail. We copped the lot. If you set your mind to it you could still have your Luke. All it takes is a little finesse.'

There was nothing to say to that piece of conceit—certainly no hope that she might be right. Luke was lost to her.

It was necessary to advise those who might need to contact her on a professional basis that she had moved out of the flat, although finding a plausible reason was something else again. In the end she simply stated she had needed a change, leaving the recipients of her phone calls to draw their own conclusions.

Picking her up on the Wednesday afternoon, Paul waited until they were clear of the city centre before saying quizzically, 'I saw Luke this morning. He seemed to think you were still at the flat. Didn't you tell your sister you were moving out?'

'I told the people I thought should know,' she said.

'Better than last time, anyway. At least I knew where you were.' He paused while he negotiated a change of lane, stepping on the accelerator to beat a truck to the junction. 'Luke said to be prepared for a surprise announcement,' he continued, ignoring the furious hooting of the horn at his rear. 'Any idea what he was talking about?'

So that was how he planned to do it, Gail thought dully. Not that it mattered one way or another. She had known the truth must come out. The last thing she would want was to deny him the faint consolation of being the one to expose her.

'Possibly,' she said.

'But you're not going to talk about it.' His glance was swift and not without sympathy. 'Is your sister going to be there too?'

'No.'

'Oh?' He waited a moment, then shrugged and laughed. 'Well, that puts paid to one theory. Now I'm really guessing!'

Gail had no intention of enlightening him. The denouement would come soon enough. She put a stop to any further conversational overtures by leaning her head back against the rest and closing her eyes, her mind forming images of the evening that lay ahead. Seeing Luke again at all would be the most difficult part. She didn't care what anyone else thought of her. That was a lie too, but it was the way she was going to play it. At least they would have a scapegoat if *Promise* failed to take off.

The billboards were already up; she had seen one that morning. National magazine coverage was to follow from tomorrow, using the same initial lay-out.

The hair and face, the expression in the sultry green eyes, they belonged to a different person. Tonight she was going to be that person for the very last time—use her as a shield against the man she loved. It was the only defence she had left.

They reached Bannerdale in time to take tea with Charlie. The latter was in high spirits, the kiss she pressed on Gail's cheek warm.

'It's looking good.' Charlie said. 'I think we're on a winner! We go out at three minutes to eight, twenty-seven past and then again bang in the middle of the ten o'clock news—peak viewing in most areas. From tomorrow we have some soap opera time too.' She smiled at Paul. 'I know you already have all the details at your finger-tips. I'm just making sure Karen has them too. It would be typical if she were the last to be told.'

'Probably,' he agreed, sounding anything but concerned. 'How many are going to be here tonight?'

'Thirty—thirty-five. Seven o'clock onwards. Luke won't be here before then himself.'

'Jeremy coming too?'

'No.' Her eyes found Gail's. 'He didn't think it would be wise considering he and Brenda just got back together again.'

Either that, or Luke had told the two of them, Gail reflected dryly. Brenda in particular would hardly feel well-disposed towards her. She had bared her soul twice over to the same person.

Later, dressing for the evening in the room she had occupied on her previous visit, she wondered at which point Luke would decide to make his announcement. If she knew him at all, he would more than likely wait until after the final slot when everyone was high on enthusiasm if not on alcohol, the better to create impact. Subconsciously she must have known how he would choose to exact retribution; there was no other reason she would have gone out and spent what she had on this dress now reflected in the mirror before her.

Flying the flag, Paul had called it. Studying the metallic silver sheath clinging so lovingly to every curve of her body, Gail could only conclude that he knew quite a lot about the way the female mind worked. Let Luke do his worst. She could take it.

People were beginning to arrive as she went downstairs. Regal in dark blue silk herself, Charlie soundly approved the silver dress. Swamped by names and faces she would never begin to tie together, Gail forced herself to relax and just go along.

She was laughing over some facile remark made by one of the men in her immediate vicinity when a prickle of awareness drew her eyes to the double doors. Like the others, Luke was wearing a dinner suit, the stark black and white superb on a man of his build. Something froze inside her as he looked across at her. Was it possible that the grey eyes had ever held that moving warmth her memory cherished so dearly?

He didn't come near her during the following half hour. At ten minutes to eight a large television set was wheeled into the drawing room, and switched on with the sound muted while the current programme drew to its end. The soft drink commercial which flashed first on to the screen was familiar enough to be semi-ignored. Next was a famous brand washing-up liquid, and then, eliciting rapt attention in all present, the moment they had been waiting for. Watching her own image, Gail felt totally detached. All that work for thirty seconds of footage. If the option on the present contract was taken up at all it was going to be just too bad because Karen Greer wasn't going to be available.

There was comment and congratulation from all

sides when it was over. Both Charlie and Paul accepted the acclaim with smiling but obvious reservations, too old hands at the game to be carried away by the spirit of the occasion. Their rejoicing would come when balance sheets started to show a profit, not before.

Luke stayed clear of the main group, spending most of the evening in conversation with the man Gail believed was the Company accountant. By ten o'clock when the news came on, she was almost ready to forestall him by making the announcement herself. The only thing giving her pause was how to get started. It was such a complicated story.

The third and final showing of the evening finished to a shower of applause. Still Luke made no move. He was leaning against the wall over by a window, a glass in his hand. Meeting the derisive gaze, seeing the curl of his upper lip, Gail knew she had reached the limit of her endurance.

Without pausing for reflection she said clearly, 'I believe you had something you wanted to say, Luke? Wouldn't now be a good time?'

For a fleeting moment, as the buzz of conversation faded, there was admiration in his eyes, wiped out as he straightened away from the wall. 'It's your triumph,' he said. 'I wouldn't rob you of it.'

'What are you two talking about?' Charlie demanded, sounding intrigued. She looked from her grandson's unyielding face to that of the girl at her side, brows drawing together. 'Karen?'

'My name is Gail,' she said without inflection. 'Karen is my twin sister.'

A general babble broke out around her as the statement registered. Charlie's expression was stupefied. 'You're joking!' she exclaimed.

'No, she isn't.' Luke hadn't moved. 'She took

Karen's place several weeks ago, before Bailey's accident. If you want to see the real one you'll need your passport.'

His grandmother was grappling with the implications, eyes widening as she searched Gail's features. 'It's fantastic!' she said with rising excitement. 'Paul, are you thinking what I'm thinking?'

'I doubt it.' His tone was ironic. 'I'd say we'd all been well and truly had.'

'And how!' The gleam in his employer's eyes in no way diminished. 'Imagine the publicity value. Just imagine it!'

Gail said softly, 'Sorry, Paul. The intention was good but it got out of hand.'

The irony remained. 'I think it might be an idea if the four of us went off somewhere quiet and thrashed out the whole story. Charlie has a point on the publicity angle.'

'Make it the three of you,' Luke intervened. 'I already know the details.'

'No, you don't.' Gail kept her tone level, her gaze steady. 'Not all of it.'

'As much as I want to know then.' He wasn't giving an inch. 'Try the library,' he added to the other man. 'I'll hold the fort through here.'

It was Charlie herself who took Gail's arm, flashing a smile round the rest of the assembly. 'Carry on enjoying yourselves, everyone. We'll be back in a little while.'

The library overlooked the rear of the house. Large enough to take a chesterfield and club chairs in addition to the study area, it offered a comfortable privacy.

'I need a drink,' Paul observed, crossing to a cabinet let in between two floor to ceiling bookshelves. 'You can get started right away,' he added over a shoulder. 'I can listen while I pour.'

Expression wry, Gail looked at the woman seated facing her. The problem wasn't so much where she started but how much she left out. Luke's involvement had to be obvious, yet there were moments in their relationship which she had no intention of disclosing to anyone.

She began hesitantly, sketching in the background in as few words as possible.

'It was only ever supposed to be for a couple of weeks at the most,' she tailed off. 'I'd no idea just where Karen was so I couldn't contact her when this job turned up. The only thing left was to go on pretending to be her and hope I could cope.'

'You certainly did that,' Charlie stated with enthusiasm. 'Especially considering you were a complete newcomer to the game. You realise, of course, that you can't work for anyone else until we decide whether we take up our option? The fee you were paid took account of that.'

'The fee was paid in the name of Karen Greer,' Paul cut in from his perch on the arm of the chesterfield. 'Are you good at forgery too?'

Gail flushed, but kept her reply level, willing to concede that he had some cause to be bitter. 'I never touched a penny of it—any of it. I had enough to live on under my own name.'

'So it's still right there in her account?'

'It was. I doubt if it still is. Karen was planning on using it before she goes back to marry her millionaire. She leaves on Saturday.'

'No hope of persuading her to postpone for a few weeks?' asked Charlie swiftly, shaking her head in answer to her own question. 'Hardly likely, is it. Millionaires don't come two a penny.' She smiled a little. 'Just a passing thought. You have a certain quality your sister lacked. I'm not sure just what it is but it came through clear enough when I picked you out of that line-up. At the time I put it down to pure technique, which was incentive enough to grant you that forty-eight hour concession.'

'Where were you anyway?' asked Paul, sounding no less brusque. 'You had Norah jumping through hoops trying to trace you!'

Gail's chin lifted a fraction. 'I don't think it's necessary for you to know that.'

His laugh was short. 'You didn't think it necessary for anybody to know much at all from the sound of it—including Luke.'

'Leave Luke to sort out his own affairs,' Charlie said firmly. 'He's more than capable. None of it really matters, when it all boils down. We'll be picking up that option, you can count on it.'

Gail bit her lip. 'I'd rather you didn't.'

'You don't have a choice.' Paul drained his glass and stood up, features hard-set. 'You accepted the terms when you signed that contract, no matter which name you used. I'm going to want you on call right here in the morning for the Press release.'

'My family don't know about all this yet,' she protested weakly. 'Can't it wait one more day?'

'No, it can't.' He was moving as he spoke, making for the door. ''Phone them, if it's that important.'

Charlie waited until they were alone before responding to the mute appeal in the green eyes, her tone not without sympathy. 'I'm afraid he's right. Strike while the iron is hot. They'll surely understand—even feel proud of you. There aren't many who could do what you did.'

There probably weren't *any* who could make the same mess of it, Gail conceded, knowing herself beaten. It was too late now to start telephoning home. Perhaps if she waited until she knew her father would have left the house in the morning and asked her stepmother to pass on the news. The latter would take it in her stride. She took most things in her stride. At least she could choose the right moment.

Lack of courage again, came the thought, but it made little difference. With no time left in which to see her father face to face, it had to be the kinder alternative.

'Would you mind if I called it a day?' she asked wearily. 'I don't think I could face any more questions tonight.'

'That's understandable.' The older woman hesitated, the struggle apparent in her eyes. 'There's just one more thing I'd like to know myself,' she added. 'Are you in love with Luke?'

Gail stiffened, then relaxed again. What did it matter? 'It's purely one-sided,' she said. 'At least, it certainly is now.' She got to her feet, desperate to be on her own. 'I'll say goodnight.'

There were a few people out in the hallway, but Luke wasn't one of them, thank God. She managed to make the stairs without being waylaid by anyone, although the glances directed her way held lively speculation.

Safe at last in her own bedroom, she shut the door and stood for a moment gathering her resources. There was a lot to think about, a lot of re-planning to be done. First and foremost, she was going to need somewhere to live if she had to stay on in town to honour her commitments. Even if Karen had not yet given notice, which was unlikely anyway, the flat would be the last place she would want to live. Finance was something else again. She could hardly ask Karen to return that portion of the fee which was supposed to cover this period of enforced rest. Still, they were aware of her situation. If she had to ask for an advance against work still to come then she would do just that.

All on a strictly impersonal basis though, she promised herself resolutely. She would do what was required of her to the best of her ability but her private life would be no one's concern but her own. She had a career now; she may as well take advantage of it. Two, perhaps three years, and she could maybe start thinking about that salon again. Her own little business; that was the answer. From now on she went all out for independence.

The warm bath was a comfort. She stayed soaking for some time, letting her mind drift back over past events. The only moments really worthy of remembrance were few and fleeting, she supposed. Certainly there was nothing to be proud of in what she had done. All the same, nothing could ever make her wholly rue the time she had spent in Luke's arms. Even now she could feel the need stirring inside her, knotting nerve and sinew as it grew. There was relief of a kind to be found, she was well aware, but it could be no substitute.

Jerkily she pressed herself to her feet, tugging out the plug with her toe as she came upright. The towels lay folded across the heated rail at the bathside. She had her hand on one of them when Luke walked into the room.

He had taken off his jacket, she noted in that moment of suspended animation. His tie too, if it came to that. The slipped upper buttons of the pristine white dress shirt revealed a triangle of dark hair. Lips dry, she just stood there gazing at him, unable to find a solitary thing to say.

The grey eyes moved over her with slow deliberation, his smile canted. 'You were right about one thing,' he observed dispassionately. 'I'd have known that body anywhere.' He took the towel from beneath her nerveless fingers and unfolded it, holding it out in sardonic invitation. 'I've been waiting nearly twenty minutes out there already so let's make it fast, shall we.'

Gail jolted herself into movement as he went out again, the anger searing through her like a live flame. There was no robe to hand, so she used another of the thick Turkish towels to form a sarong when she was dried, tucking in the ends with a savage twist. It hardly mattered under the circumstances, but she wasn't going out there naked.

Luke had not suffered the same reservations. He was lying out on the bed when she did go through, hands clasped comfortably behind his head, one knee raised. 'Get that off and come on over here,' he said.

Gail stayed where she was at the bathroom door, the rage consuming her. 'What do you think I am?' she demanded contemptuously.

'I *know* what you are,' came the level response. 'I also know what you're capable of being. I'm claiming a little interest on account, that's all. You'd hardly deny me that much, would you?'

'I wouldn't give you the right time!'

'Wrong character.' His tone mocked. 'You wouldn't have made that mistake a few days ago—but then you hardly need to separate the two halves anymore, do you? You're a clever little actress, I have to give you that. There aren't many women who can appeal to a man on two totally different levels.'

'Not *so* different surely,' she retorted, borrowing the same inflection. 'You'd have had me in bed that very first time I came to your place if I'd given you half a chance!'

'True,' he agreed. 'As I said once before, it would take another man to know what I'm talking about.' He

came suddenly upright, swinging his feet to the floor.
'We're going to finish this my way.'

Gail made no move as he came towards her. She had
seen him like this a dozen times or more, yet the
mood was hardly the same. Heart hammering against
her ribs, she said huskily, 'You won't get anything out
of it.'

He put out a hand and yanked the towel open,
allowing it to drop in a heap at her feet. 'Want to bet?'

His mouth was ruthless. Hauled up hard against the
lean, muscular body, Gail set her mind to staying rigid
and unyielding, clenching her hands into fists to stop
them from moving up from her sides. Only no amount
of willpower could damp down the heat, no stiffening
of limb hide the tremors slowly building. At some
point, without quite knowing when, she found herself
kissing him back, starting to move against him in the
slow and subtle caress her body knew so well. It had
been a lifetime since she had known his closeness, his
hardness, the scent of his skin in her nostrils. If this
was going to be their final hour then let it be a worthy
one.

He took her right there on the soft, thick carpet, in
total command the whole way through.

'You're going to remember tonight,' he said
roughly, watching her face as she struggled to regain
her breath. 'We're both going to remember it. That
last night we spent together you were everything any
man could want in his bed. That's the way I want you
now—the way I'm going to *have* you now! I don't care
how long it takes, do you hear me?'

There was no reply she could make that would
change his present attitude, she knew. He had to get
the anger out of his system first, and there was only
one way. She reached for him hungrily, passionately,
seeing the ice start to melt from his eyes, the flame

spring to life. No more pretence, either with him or
with herself. This was her need too.

The dawn chorus was in full spate when she awoke.
She was lying on her side facing the other empty
pillow. So that was that, she thought dully. All done
and dusted. He wouldn't be back again.

There was movement from the direction of the
window. When she rolled she could see him sitting
there, profile outlined against the pale grey light. He
was wearing shirt and trousers, the former unbuttoned
at the throat.

'I thought you'd gone,' she murmured very softly
after a moment.

'I should have done,' he said, not turning his head.
'I've been sitting here for the past hour trying to
persuade myself to walk out of that door.'

Gail hardly dared say it. 'Only?'

'Only I don't have what it takes to give you up.' He
was looking at her now, lips faintly curved. 'So
supposing we start over? Does it appeal?'

She came up on an elbow, trying to match his calm.
'You don't have any trust left in me. How could it
work?'

'We shan't know unless we try it.' The pause
seemed to stretch interminably. 'So?' he asked.

It would be easy to just say yes and hope for the
best. Too easy. She sought for the right words. 'Will
you let me try to explain why I did what I did first,'
she said. 'It really wasn't the way you thought.'

It was difficult to see his expression in this half
light. His voice gave little away either. 'Which way
was it?'

She took a moment to collect herself, not at all sure
it was going to be possible to make him understand.
'Initially I wanted to pay you back for what happened

up at the cottage,' she admitted, and then in sudden self-insight, 'No, not because of what happened but because you wouldn't believe I wasn't what you thought I was.'

'Sounds complicated,' Luke remarked in a dry note. 'Are you sure you wouldn't rather leave it alone?'

She made a helpless little gesture. 'The only thing I can say is that once I got started I just kept getting in deeper and deeper. I suppose, basically, I felt I needed experience to attract you, and I didn't have enough as myself. Pretending to be Karen gave me the confidence to make advances I'd never have dared to make otherwise.'

He considered her thoughtfully. 'So why the follow-up after I came north? I'd have been no wiser if you hadn't taken me up on that offer.'

'It was just physical for you where my Karen half was concerned. I wanted more than that.' Gail made herself go on. 'I was in love with you by then, and not thinking all that straight. I just lived from day to day—sometimes even minute to minute.' Her laugh was shaky. 'Have you any idea what it was like trying to live two lives at once?'

'Have you any idea what it was like to see the real Karen walk in last Sunday morning and realise you'd been playing me every which way?'

'I can imagine.' There was a pause, then she lifted her shoulders. 'No, I don't suppose I can. Not wholly. The worst of it was I'd already decided I had to get out of your life completely. I was going to write you a letter—a full confession. You'd have received it tomorrow, by which time I'd planned to be far away. Not that it would have worked out anyway considering the fact that I'd still have been stuck with that contract. I was an absolute idiot all the way through!'

'I made my own contribution when I snatched the

wrong girl.' Luke wasn't exactly smiling but he looked close. 'You weren't the only one turning a blind eye either. There were certain things that bothered me about you and your so-called sister, only I never let myself get round to making any in-depth comparisons. Maybe I didn't really want to know.' He paused, studying her quizzically. 'Do I take it you still have some feeling left for me after the way I treated you last night?'

Green eyes took on a deeper hue. 'Was it supposed to turn me off?'

'It was supposed to put you down,' he said on an ironic note. 'Only I got just a little off-track.'

Gail said softly, 'Would you fancy trying again?'

'You read minds too?' He came slowly to his feet, fingers sliding the buttons of his shirt as he moved towards the bed, the expression in his eyes all she needed to see. 'We've a lot of making up to do. Think you're up to it at this hour?'

'If you are.' She was laughing, loving him, holding out her arms as he shed his clothing, the relief lofting through her. 'Anytime you're ready.'

It had been good last night, but it was wonderful this morning. Held safe and secure in those firm, strong arms while her senses slowed their gallop, Gail still found it difficult to credit that her problems were actually over.

'Do you still feel the same way about having a working wife?' she asked sleepily. 'Because I don't think Charlie is going to do you any favours.'

'From her I wouldn't expect any.' Luke kissed her temple. 'I only objected to finding my future wife a job, not the fact of her having one at all. You're heading for the top, and I wouldn't stand in your way. Maybe someday you'll have other commitments, only that isn't going to be yet for a while. I'll share you in the day but I'm damned if I'll share you at night!'

'We didn't even get married yet,' she reminded him, and felt him smile.

'Yes, but with you things have a way of getting out of hand. I'm putting my marker on the next couple of years at least.'

Two years. By then she would probably have had enough of this career business anyway, she thought contentedly. There were a lot of explanations and apologies still to come, and she couldn't say she was looking forward to them, but Luke would see her through. They were together again, and nothing else mattered but that.

ROMANCE

Variety is the spice of romance

Each month, Mills & Boon publish new romances. New stories about people falling in love. A world of variety in romance — from the best writers in the romantic world. Choose from these titles in May.

CAPRICORN MAN Jacqueline Gilbert
BUSHRANGER'S MOUNTAIN Victoria Gordon
BIG SUR Elizabeth Graham
THE OBJECT OF THE GAME Vanessa James
TAKEN OVER Penny Jordan
HOSTAGE Madeleine Ker
DARK OBSESSION Valerie Marsh
TRUST IN TOMORROW Carole Mortimer
MODEL OF DECEPTION Margaret Pargeter
DOUBLE DECEPTION Kay Thorpe

On sale where you buy paperbacks. If you require further information or have any difficulty obtaining them, write to: Mills & Boon Reader Service, PO Box 236, Thornton Road, Croydon, Surrey CR9 3RU, England.

Mills & Boon
the rose of romance

 **ROMANCE**

Next month's romances from Mills & Boon

Each month, you can choose from a world of variety in romance with Mills & Boon. These are the new titles to look out for next month.

DON'T PLAY GAMES Emma Darcy
A WORLD OF DIFFERENCE Sandra Field
AGE OF CONSENT Victoria Gordon
OUTCAST LOVERS Sarah Holland
TIME FUSE Penny Jordan
ACAPULCO MOONLIGHT Marjorie Lewty
ECLIPSE OF THE HEART Mary Lyons
DREAMS TO KEEP Leigh Michaels
IMPASSE Margaret Pargeter
A SECRET PLEASURE Flora Kidd

Buy them from your usual paperback stockist, or write to: Mills & Boon Reader Service, P.O. Box 236, Thornton Rd, Croydon, Surrey CR9 3RU, England. Readers in South Africa - write to: Mills & Boon Reader Service of Southern Africa, Private Bag X3010, Randburg, 2125.

Mills & Boon
the rose of romance

Twice as romantic.

'Hidden in the Flame' is a compelling, involving story of love and revolution in South America, and twice the length of a Mills & Boon romance.

Anne Mather is a best-selling author, world-renowned for more than 90 romantic novels.

'Hidden in the Flame' is published on 10th May. Twice the romance for just £2.95.

The Rose of Romance

The perfect holiday romance.

ACT OF BETRAYAL
Sara Craven

MAN HUNT
Charlotte Lamb

YOU OWE ME
Penny Jordan

LOVERS IN THE AFTERNOON
Carole Mortimer

Have a more romantic holiday this summer with the
Mills & Boon holiday pack.

Four brand new titles, attractively packaged for only £4.40.

The holiday pack is published on the 14th June. Look out for it
where you buy Mills & Boon.

The Rose of Romance